JENSON

STRONG MANOR Book 1

KATHI S. BARTON

This is a work of fiction. Names, characters, places, and incidents are products of the author's imagination or are used fictitiously and are not to be construed as real. Any resemblance to actual events, locations, organizations, or persons, living or dead, is entirely coincidental.

World Castle Publishing, LLC
Pensacola, Florida
Copyright © Kathi S. Barton 2022
Hardback ISBN: 9798352791967
Paperback ISBN: 9781958336700
eBook ISBN: 9781958336717
First Edition World Castle Publishing, LLC, September 19, 2022
http://www.worldcastlepublishing.com
Cover: Karen Fuller
Editor: Karen Fuller

Chapter 1

Jade sat down at one of the empty booths and looked at the album that had been given to her just this morning when she'd shown up to work. It was her last day here at the restaurant that she'd spent more than half her life working at. She looked up when someone sat across from her. It was Ms. Bruce, Ms. B for short, the restaurant owner—up until last month and a better mother to her than her own.

"You're going to miss this old place." Jade said that she would. "Don't you be looking for another job waiting tables, young lady. You get out there and see the world, then you go on and find yourself a job that is more suited to that education that you got."

Ms. B was the nicest person in the world. She'd not only taken good care of her, but she'd also been there when she needed her. Her husband of sixty-three years had passed away ten years ago, and it had hurt her as much as it had Ms. B. He was sorely missed by both.

"Mom called me yesterday, well, yesterday morning, but I didn't call her back until later. She said that she was going to come here to see me about something. I told her that I wasn't going to be around after today. That upset her. She said that I was ungrateful." Ms. B. looked thoughtful and then asked her if she thought that she was going to want some money. "More than likely. I don't give her anything anymore. While she's not been as horrible of a mother to me as she might have been had I stuck around, she's just not anyone that I want in my life anymore."

"No, you'd not need that around you anymore." Ms. B opened the album to the first page, to the day that she'd started working for her place. "I wish - I'd have known about how she was with you back then. I might well have taken you to my home." She clasped Jade's hand for a gentle squeeze. "But you were, as you are now, very closed mouth about your personal life."

"I don't have a personal life that you don't know about." They both laughed. "I can't believe I've worked here for the last twelve years. I mean, it doesn't seem possible. I've met so many people in all these years. And now you're going to be moving away, and I'll only see you once in a while instead of all the time now. I will miss this place and you."

As they were looking through the photo album, they talked about the pictures that were in it. The Strong family, a huge part of the community, were in a lot of them. Jade had waited on the elderly couple every Sunday for the last ten or so years. She thought they were a nice couple.

"The couple had been coming into my place since my mom first opened. Bringing in their child to eat with them, then as he grew older, they'd bring in a couple of his friends. After he married his wife, years later, they would begin to bring in their child to eat with their grandparents. They were the nicest family I've ever known. Then Bar got married himself, and they never came around anymore. Just Mr. and Mrs. Strong."

"When her husband passed away, I thought for sure that she'd not come in anymore. They were such a wonderful couple. I'm sure that there wasn't another couple that loved each other as much as the two of them did." Mrs. Strong, the elder, had passed away not long after Jade had graduated from high school at fourteen. Jade smiled as she remembered the woman. "She gave me a thousand dollars for my graduation gift. I tried to tell her that it was too much, but she wouldn't hear of it. Then a few days later, she had a stroke that took her life. I miss them."

"I do as well." When one of the Strong men came into the diner, Jade just watched him as Ms. B. got up to wait on him.

Jade didn't know them by name; however, she knew the names that they'd been given. Just not who was who. There were six of them, all men of worth. They would come in once a week, on Sundays, to have a piece of pie like their grandmother did to commemorate her passing. She often wondered how they had any idea what she had liked to eat as they had only started coming around after she had passed away.

Jenson was the oldest son. He was a big man,

and she thought that he was some sort of politician. It wasn't in her to keep track of who was who in the political world, so she didn't know for sure what it was he did.

Clay was the next oldest. She knew that he was a teacher of something but was not sure what he taught. Ms. B told her once that he was head of a science department that landed rovers on other planets. Again, it wasn't something that she had had time to look at because of her education, as well as working full time.

The next two, she didn't know all that well. Only that Barkley and Barton were twins who didn't look the least bit alike. At least to her. And that women fawned all over them, hoping for a piece of the action that would eventually end up with them knocked up with one of their kids to be a part of the very wealthy Strong family. Christ, women like those gold-diggers gave other women bad names.

Maverick was next. He was a financial advisor that kept the Strong family in money. She wasn't sure, but she had heard that they had all the money in the world, so his job seemed, to her anyway, kind of stupid. But then, people thought that hers was as well.

Trevor, someone that she had known a little, had gone to college when she had. At fourteen, it had been difficult for her to get around campus. She couldn't drive yet and couldn't afford a new bike at the time, but he had been nice to her when she'd been stranded in the snow with Mr. B's old bike that had been broken and taken her to her building. Even after her class, he'd been outside waiting in his wonderfully warm car to take her home. She'd only seen him since then in here at the restaurant having pie with his brothers. He had never really acknowledged her again. She didn't have a clue what it was that he did but didn't care either. They were all so far out of her league that she was sure they were on a different planet.

Jade had managed to graduate first in her class with her bachelor's degree as well as second in her class with a doctorate as a medical engineer. Being only seventeen, when she finished her doctorate, Jade finished up her medical degree to be in the hospital to get more education as a physician. She'd had to work from the diner the first year of her job because they couldn't allow her in the building until she was eighteen. Even then, they had been accommodating to her, setting up a good computer as well as a laptop so that she could do the work she was very good at, as it turned out. She worked in a lab environment most of the time, developing medical solutions and was involved in research as well as developing and testing medical devices. While she could be counted on to fix such testing machines, she rarely did that anymore as she was good at her other job.

"Are you Miss Anderson?" Looking up at Jenson, she said that she was. Right off the bat, she didn't care for him or his tone in asking her who she was. "I know you know who my grandmother is. And I'm sure you know she passed away a few years ago. My family and I are having a get-together to remember her by. Grandma asked if you could be there too. It won't be a big celebration but just a couple of hundred people." As he straightened his tie, Jade inwardly seethed. "We'll expect you there on time and with a nice dress on. I'm not kidding you when I tell you not to embarrass the family with whatever you think you might be wearing. So be respectable and nice looking." She decided to ignore his comment about her clothing and smiled instead.

"I thought you said it wouldn't be a big celebration. That's a lot of people." He looked pissed for a second time, and she asked him when it was. After he told her, she shook her head. "I have to work that day. But I do thank you for so politely asking me to attend."

"You're not coming?" He looked as if he couldn't believe she'd rejected his invitation. She said no, not even if she didn't have to work. She took some satisfaction at the anger that flashed in his eyes. "Why not? Are you too good for us? My grandmother wanted you there, and you'll have to make other arrangements for someone else to wait on your tables before I allow you to turn her only request down."

"Allow? I've got news for you, mister. Last time I checked, you didn't sign my paycheck, nor are you my daddy. I guess it sucks to be you. I'm not going. I have to work. Some of us have to make a living as we're not handed everything on a silver platter." He looked at the others that had been sitting with him before glaring back at her. She knew she'd pissed him off, but she didn't care. Good. It served him right, but she still needed to keep her own temper in check. "I've been a waitress for the last twelve years, Mr. Strong. You don't frighten me in the least little bit. I'm busy. I'm not going."

She stood up, and he pushed her back in the seat. So much for keeping her temper in check. The sound of scraping chairs had her up and hitting the man square in the face before she could think that the others might be coming to his rescue. If the others were going to come and hurt her, she was going to take care of this asshole first and foremost.

Jade didn't just punch him in the face but knocked him back on his ass, where he broke one of the few tables in the middle of the diner when one of the spindly legs shattered. The splintered table leg had not only broken off but entered his leg from the back of his thigh and came out through the top. She immediately went into physician mode.

"Call an ambulance. Also, the police." Ms. B was right there with his brothers, and she had her get everything she'd need to make sure that the man didn't bleed out. Jenson shoved her away from his bleeding leg, and she'd had about enough of his shit. "Listen, you mother fucker. You either let me help you, or you die right here. Then your brothers can live a stress-free life without you, and I have no doubt that you stress everyone out by your ordering them around. Lay back. Shut the fuck up and let me do my job."

While waiting on the ambulance to come for the dumbass, she had tied off his leg wound and wrapped the wound with the wood still inside of it. Explaining, mostly for her calmness, she said everything she was doing and why. By the time the ambulance was pulling up out in front of the diner, she was ready to call it a day. Instead, she was asked to go in the ambulance with him to the hospital so that she could tell them what was going on.

"I can't." One of the medics, Peter, told her that she'd done a great job at keeping him calm and she snorted. "He's a prick."

One of the brothers laughed and agreed with her. She didn't want to engage in talking to him, so when they were going to follow his brother into the hospital, Trevor stayed behind to talk to her. He asked her if she was all right.

"I am. Thank you for asking. You should go see what he needs." Trevor said that he'd let him know if he needed anything. "Of that, I have no doubt. He touched me first. Not to mention he was very rude to me. Ordering me around like I'm a simpleton. He even told me that I was going to his grandmother's memorial and that I was to clean up and wear nice clothing."

"I'd like to say that this is unusual for him, but it's not. Lately, we all avoid him. Are you going to come to the memorial?" She said that she did have to work. "It was my understanding that this place and the acres around it have been sold, and this place is closing up."

"It is. This isn't what I do for a living. Although it did put me through college, I have other resources that I depend on. Besides, I don't think that even after what your brother said to me, I'd have all that much in common with anyone there. I do have to work, however." He nodded, and she began cleaning up the mess that she'd made. Trevor helped. "I can do this, Mr. Strong. Just, well, I don't want to be rude, but you should get to the hospital to see your brother. If you could perhaps give me a heads up if he plans on suing me, I'd like that very much."

"He won't sue you." He sounded so firm on the idea that she almost believed him. Almost. She didn't think that Jenson would have any trouble suing her for him being a jackass to her. "May I call you Jade? I remember you in college. I gave you a ride once, if I remember. You were a kid back then."

"I was." He just nodded when she didn't have anything else to say to him. "Mr. Strong—" He told her to call him Trevor. "Since I doubt that we'll see each other after this, Mr. Strong, I'd like to thank your family for the invitation to your grandmother's celebration. I did love her and her husband, but I do have to work, so if you'd tell whoever is in charge that I thank them for the invite, I'll be going home now."

Picking up her photo album, she left the diner. Jade could still hear him laughing as she got through the door and out into the cold. The Strong men were nuts, was all she could think about as she waited for her car to warm up enough that it wouldn't die when put into gear. Stupid men. They were all nuts.

~*~

Jenson startled awake and sat up. This caused him to cry out in pain, and he had a few seconds of wondering what the fuck had happened. Then he looked at his leg, and his temper, not all that maintained lately, flared up when he remembered the waitress hitting him.

"You should be ashamed of yourself." He looked over at his mom, who was knitting. The way that her needles were clacking together made him realize that she was as pissed off as he was. Without looking up, she continued. "What made you think that you could talk to anyone like you did that young woman? To tell her to make sure that she was dressed nicely? Then on top of that, you shoved her into the seat like she was nothing but an errant child."

She finally looked up at him. "She said that she wasn't coming to grandmother's celebration and that she had to work. I told her to find someone else to wait at her table. That's all." His mother clicked her tongue at him. "Why are you mad at me? I'm the one that's in the hospital. Not her."

"You're only alive because she, a mere waitress, according to you, was there to save your butt. Did you know that when she knocked you back—justifiably too, from what I've heard—that the splintered table leg nicked your artery? That had she not been the one to tie off your leg so that you'd not bleed out, that you'd be dead now?" He asked her what she was getting at. "What do you mean, what am I getting at? I thought I was being clear on what I'm telling you. And you should have read the report on the employees that work at the diner before behaving like an idiot when you were told to *ask*, not tell her to come to the celebration. What is wrong with you of late? You've been snipping and snapping at everyone, including me, for the last several months."

"I have a lot on my mind." She asked him what that might be. "It's stuff with work. I've been working on things that aren't coming to fruition as quickly as I wanted them to. Not to mention this thing with dad."

"Your father? What's he done that has you so upset? This might well have slipped your mind, Jenson, but we're both old enough that we don't need a sitter anymore. Not to mention needing our son to babysit us." He said that he knew that. "Do you? I'm not so sure about a great many things with you of late. Why is it that Trevor refuses to talk to you? Or, for that matter, Barkley and Clay? What about Maverick? You've pissed off a great many people. As I'm sure was your plan."

"I didn't want to bother you and dad with

what I have going on." She just glared at him. His leg was aching right now, and he didn't want to say the wrong thing to his mother. "Did you know that the money that we set aside for the new school programs is missing? Also, the high school was supposed to have received their football uniforms for this season, and they've not been delivered."

"And?" He asked her if she didn't think that was wrong. "Wrong? Not really. The school board received an email from the company making the uniforms that the material that they used to put the uniforms together wasn't being delivered in a reasonable timeframe. So they made a deal with the school to not only make their basketball jerseys and shorts for half price, but they were also going to give them a huge discount next time the school orders for their mistake."

"No one told me that." She asked him if he'd asked anyone about it. "I was going to, then other things started popping up too."

"The before and after school program, I'm assuming." He was hurting now, so he only nodded at his mother. "Call the nurse, Jenson. We can have this conversation at any time. However, I will try to ease your mind by telling you that they've not set up the programs because they don't have enough volunteers to work the time slots they were planning to run them with. The money isn't missing but being put to good use on other projects that were also on the list that—call the flipping nurse, Jenson."

He did. And when someone at the desk finally answered his call, he was nearly ready to beg them for something for pain. Jenson felt like his leg had been torn off and slapped back on. As soon as the nurse gave him an IV injection of pain meds, Jenson felt his entire body simply shut down. The pain wasn't gone, but it certainly was a good deal easier to deal with.

At some point, he must have dozed off. His mother was gone, but his dad was sitting there working on a crossword puzzle. When he asked him where mom was, dad told him that she'd gone home to get a shower.

"I don't need you guys to sit around with me while I'm here. I'm sure you have better things to do than to watch me sleep." Dad just looked at him, confusion written all over his face. "Dad, I'm not being rude, but I'm perfectly capable of being in the hospital by myself."

"I'm sure you are. But you almost lost your life, and I began to realize that I needed to hang out with my sons more often than I had been. Watching you sleep, to me anyway, is better than planning your funeral." Jenson felt his face heat up. "That young woman that put you in your place, I've been doing some research on her. You're an idiot compared to this young woman. I'm not going to go into details with you because, frankly, I don't think you deserve it. However, I will tell you that you need to get your head out of your ass and stop judging people for what you think and see them for what they are."

"You do understand that I'm the victim here? I'm the one in the hospital with my leg hurting." His dad asked him if he thought he was justified in treating Jade the way he had. "I was told to make sure she was invited to the gathering with grandma. I did that, and she hit me. Then on top of that, she put me in the hospital with a messed up leg."

Dad stood up and looked at him. At that moment, for the first time in his life, Jenson saw disappointment on his face. All of it was directed solely at him. When he left his room, not even bothering to tell him goodbye or even to say that he loved him, Jenson was left alone in the room to think.

Usually, Jenson was never one to second guess what he did or said to someone. But right now, he was thinking of how he had treated Jade. He hadn't been going to admit to anyone, including himself, that he'd been in the wrong. But from all accounts, she had saved his life even after he'd been a total jerk to her. However, he tried to think of it being her fault for hitting him and telling him no — a word that he simply hated to be told — he'd done her wrong. More than that, he'd been a total ass to her and thought that perhaps he had deserved how his family was treating him.

Picking up his cell phone, sitting on the little table by his bed, he called his attorney. Jenson wanted to get a full background check on this woman and berated himself for not doing it sooner. As soon as Holly answered the phone, he told her what he needed.

"You mean Jade Anderson?" He said that was her. "Yes, well, I can tell you anything you want to know about her. She and I are cousins. However, I don't think that you're going to be overly impressed.

Jade told me what you did to her in the diner the day before yesterday."

Jenson hadn't even realized that he'd been in the hospital for two days. Asking her what she'd heard, she told him what his parents had told him. That not only had he deserved being knocked on his ass, but he should have been nicer.

She said she'd get back to him on what she could find for him on a non-personal level. While he liked Holly a great deal, and she was an amazing attorney, he wasn't thrilled that she was talking to him as if he was stupid. And she had. Telling him that he needed to curb his temper before someone took him to the task. Again. Also that he needed to stop looking at people like they were out to get something from him.

"Not all people are the same, you know." He didn't get a chance to answer her when she started again. "Leave Jade alone. She doesn't need any more bitterness in her life, and for someone who has it all, you're about as bitter as anyone I've ever met." When she hung up, he just laid there.

What was wrong with people lately? He'd just been warned off by a woman that he didn't particularly care for right now. Instead of waiting to find out what little Holly might be giving him, he searched for Jade Anderson. In seconds there were so many hits on his search than he could have imagined.

She'd graduated from high school at thirteen. Not unusual, he supposed as he might have thought. He had graduated at the same age. He was sure that all his family had. However, where they differed was that she'd gone straight into college while he'd waited until he was eighteen to go back to higher education.

Not only did Jade have a doctorate in her chosen field as a medical engineer, but she also had a bachelor's in math and science. She was a certified doctor that volunteered at the homeless shelter and had been at ground zero at a few disasters around the world. As he read over her accomplishments, one thing occurred to him. There were never any pictures of the young woman in any of the articles, and—he found this one to be strange—there were never any quotes from her about anything she'd done. Not even to say that she had done this all on her own.

There were some articles about a Hilda Anderson he found as well. Jenson couldn't know for sure, but he thought the woman was Jade's mother. There were several places when she'd been interviewed about Jade where she didn't have anything good to say about the younger woman. One quote that he thought was very telling was when Hilda complained that her little girl had abandoned her at the age of thirteen. He couldn't figure out how that had come to pass. Children didn't normally abandon their parents. Usually, it was the other way around.

The more he read about Hilda, the more impressed he was with Jade. To have had a mother like she had, while not abusive but surely toxic, and accomplish the things that she had was a miracle. Not only had she gotten herself educated, but she had worked hard at not having to have loans that would have come due after she had graduated.

When his dinner was brought to him that night, he had also been given a file from Holly. She didn't stay, telling him that she had a date with her husband, but she told him that if he wanted more, she could get it for him first thing on Monday morning. He'd been so wrapped up in what he'd been reading that he'd not even realized that it was time for her to be off work.

Dinner didn't look that bad, but it wasn't what he might have ordered from a nice restaurant. As he was eating the soup and sandwich, he realized that he'd been wrong. The food was much better than he might have gotten, even at a five-star restaurant. With his belly full and his medications kicking in, he was ready to relax with the file he'd been given before sleeping. It was nearly midnight when he got through the first part of the file folder.

Hilda is the mother of Jade. Hilda also had a brother, Jacob, Holly's father, that was a good deal better at everything than his older sister had been. Everything that Jacob touched seemed to turn to gold. While Hilda went from one disaster to the next with only the clothing on her back. She'd had Jade when she'd been barely sixteen, and while everyone around her wanted to put her up for adoption, Hilda had kept the baby. The notes that were in Holly's handwriting told him that her aunt had held onto the child because everyone was telling her that she was too immature to raise her. 'Of course, it looked like they were right, but that was when the story started to make me think that Jade had been the mature one in their little dynamics.'

Jade, at the age of two, had learned how to read. Once she had that under her belt, she began making sure that the bills had been paid and on time also that she and her mother had food on the table nightly. Since they were living in government-subsidized housing, the only real thing that they should have been paying for was their food. But Hilda had gotten cable, a cell phone, as well as a plethora of other items that, with no income coming in, soon were turned off. That was when Jade had gotten a job for herself.

By the time Jade was six, she had two jobs working around the neighborhood that earned her enough cash to pay for her supplies for school as well as anything extra — like a coat Holly had told him to walk to school in.

Cleaning houses at her age couldn't have been easy on the child, but she did it until she turned thirteen. Then she'd gone to apply for a job at the diner where he'd seen her a few days ago.

She was now, twelve years later, twenty-four years old with a better education than he had. Not only that, she was one of the few people in the world that could break down just about any machine that had ever been made and repair it. Even if she'd never seen the machine while it had been working. Along with having a medical degree. Jade was well respected at any hospital or field operation that she worked at by all her peers and clients as well. He couldn't have been more impressed with her than if he'd been with anyone else in his life. Christ, he'd been a real shit, he realized.

Picking up his cell again, he called the diner. While it wasn't difficult to find the number, calling it made him feel horrible for the way that he'd treated someone that was much nicer than he might have been in that Jade had saved his life. When the phone was answered, he thought about hanging up but plunged forward.

"My name is Jenson Strong. I was wondering if there was some way that I could get in touch with Jade Anderson." There was a long pause. He decided he had better continue before they hung up on him. "I know that I treated her badly, and I wanted to make it up to her. At the very least, to tell her that I'm sorry and that I was a shithead."

"She's upstairs. Let me go and see if she'll come down to talk to you. But don't hold your breath on it. She's working right now and gets upset when she is interrupted. All right?" He said he'd hold on. After what seemed an eternity but only about five minutes, the woman came back on the phone. "Jade told me to tell you that she'll be at the hospital in the morning for an install and that she'll talk to you after that. Also, she said to tell you that if you want to know anything about her, you don't need to go through the hoops that you are. Just ask her."

"Yes, you're right. She's right. I'll do that." She asked him if he needed anything else. After telling her no, he thought of something. "Does Jade like coffee?"

"Nope. Just water. Nothing but water. The colder, the better." He heard someone else speaking and then spoke to him in a hurried voice. "Mr. Strong, we're kind of busy here. If there's nothing else, I'm hanging up now."

The phone went dead when he told her that he didn't need anything else. Putting his cell phone down, his nurse came into the room. Everyone here had been so good to him that he wondered if they'd heard how he'd treated one of their own. While wondering, that didn't mean he was stupid enough to ask her about it. Instead, he took his meds for the evening and settled on the bed. Jensen, if he was honest with himself, was embarrassed at how terrible of a person he'd been.

Chapter 2

Jade wasn't sure that these people watching her had any idea as to what she was doing. Not that it mattered, she supposed. They wanted to watch her install the robotic arm on the off chance they had any questions about its installation. She could answer their questions about how it worked, how easy it was to use even. Hell, she thought, she could even show them how it operated on a patient.

"Jade, can you tell us how much this will save us over, say, the next ten years?" She turned to the president of the hospital and asked him what he meant. "Well, I know the price that we've paid for this arm. Even how much we're going to be paying for the insurance on it. But what will it save us in the long term in getting more and more patients helped with it?"

"I'm not sure what you mean. However, if you're asking me in the long term if more people will be saved, I would have to tell you that it would depend on the person using the machine. Will it help people recover quicker? Yes. After weeks as there will be a smaller incision needed to cut to take care of any issue that it's being used for. But the money end of it? No, I have no part in that at all. That would be up to you and your hospital." He asked her how much she thought they could charge per operation. "I have no idea, Mr. Pauly. My job today is to install it and put out a link so that whoever needs to use it comes to some of the classes that are being held to know the ins and outs of the process."

"You're not answering my questions. Whom do I need to talk to so that I might get a clearer picture than what you're not telling me?" She looked at the others in the room and saw one of the Strong men in the group. Whatever the hell he wanted, she wasn't going to be bullied into anything today. "I want to know how much we can charge for each operation.

Surely, they let you know that when they tell you to come here and install it. Right?"

"No. As I've said to you a couple of times now, I have nothing to do with that. I just design the machines then install them if no one else is—"

The laughter from Mr. Pauly cut her off. "You? You want me to believe that you came up with the idea to make this machine. No, that's not possible. First of all, you'd have to be fairly smart, and while you might be a little smart, it takes a great deal of brain power to come up with something this delicate." She just stared at him. "Also, I don't know if you're aware of this or not. This hospital isn't going to let you come here and blow wind up our butts about things that aren't true. You've wasted enough of our time by not answering my questions."

She started to walk away. It was that or knock the man on his ass. Before she could do either, Strong, she thought his name might have been Clay, cleared his throat before speaking. She turned her back to the group of them and began working on putting the last pieces of the machine together.

"Mr. Pauly, that was extremely rude of you, don't you think? I mean, why would you assume that she was lying about designing this piece? You have to have a better reason than just assuming she's not smart." She wanted to tell Clay or whomever his name was that she didn't need his help when he laughed and spoke again. "My brother made that mistake with a woman once, and it ended up him nearly losing his life. Not that it was her fault at all, but assuming that someone is too dumb to come up with something like this robotic arm will have all kinds of people breathing down your back for being a little shit."

"Clay, or Mr. Strong, I didn't see you there." Mr. Pauly backed away from her when she stood up. Jade was just a little over six feet tall, and Mr. Pauly was probably only about five foot two or three. "Jade? Are you going to finish this project sometime today? I've other meetings to attend today."

"No one invited you to come down here and harass me in the first place. If you feel you've wasted your time being here, watching my every move, that's all on you." She loaded up the tools that she'd also designed to work on projects like this one and lifted her tool bag. "Mr. Pauly, don't call my direct office when you have trouble with this machine. Not that I think you will, but *I* won't help you. I don't care whom you have in your pocket to make me… how did you put it? Oh, yeah, jump when you say so. But you can call the line that everyone else uses that calls in, and they'll be glad to send someone else out to take care of issues for you."

It took her a good ten minutes to calm down after putting the tools in her truck. Christ, people got nastier every day, and she wasn't going to go out on calls anymore if no one couldn't respect her. At the knock on her window, she rolled it down and looked at Clay as he smiled at her.

"Did you forget you're going to talk to Jansen today?" She said that she was currently debating on whether or not she was in a good enough frame of mind to talk to him. "I can understand that. Mr. Pauly is in trouble with the board. Not for just today with you but over a lot of sexist things he's been saying."

"Why do you care?" He just shrugged. "Whatever. Mr. Strong, is there a reason that you felt you had to watch over my installation of the robot or were you wanting to be there when I talked to your brother?"

"I didn't know you were in the hospital until

I was told that Pauly was berating someone in the operating room about your robot. I only came to pull him away if it got out of hand. Seeing you there and handling him like a pro was a perk. And yes, I'm going to go with you to see Jenson. My mom sent me. She and my dad are pissed off at Jenson for the way that he treated you. I'm there to kick his ass. Unless you beat me to it." He reached into her tool bag and pulled out one of the newest tools she'd come up with. He examined it and felt its weight before nodding his approval. "I like this. It has a great deal of power without being too heavy. I can see this being used for a great many applications at my job. Do you sell these too?"

"It's only a prototype. If you want to take it and see if it works for you, then you can. Just make sure that you let me know, *me,* not the others that work for me, if it needs any improvements or to be tweaked for what you might need it for. There are three lithium batteries there too that you can take as well as the charger." He thanked her and took the bag out of her truck. "I sort of know what you do for a living. I have other tools that might suit you better. Non-arcing tools that wouldn't cause you any trouble while in space. If you'd like, I can also send some of those to your office as well."

"I'd like that. I have to admit to you that it had never occurred to me to make the tools that I could use. That's very clever and efficient. But I have a feeling that you have no troubles at all looking outside the hardware store for getting things that work for you." She didn't know what to say to that, so she didn't. "All right. I'm parked right over there. If you'd wait on me to put these in my car, I'd appreciate it. My mom is depending on me to make Jenson behave."

"I can take care of myself." He said that he was well aware of that, but Jenson needed to get his ass out of his head. "Yes, he does. I would say that most rich people are like that. Thinking that people are beneath them."

"You just tell it like it is, don't you? I love it." He was still laughing when they made their way to the elevators to head up to the fifth floor. "As for lumping rich people all into the same group, I want you to know that I have done that myself. Being the rich shit that people think that I am. But I won't again. Will you have dinner with me after this meeting with my brother?"

"No." She got off the elevator on the right floor. Walking down to the idiots' room. Clay was laughing hard by the time she was standing outside Mr. Strong's room and was dismayed to find that not only were his parents there, but so were his other brothers. She didn't want to be here anymore than Jenson looked like he wanted them there. "I should come back."

They all told her no, to stay, including Jenson. She was offered a chair to sit on but declined. Jade didn't figure she'd be here long enough to get comfy, so she stood next to the bed where Jenson was. Then they went back to what she could only assume was arguing.

They were good at it too. No one cursed. She thought that was because both parents were present. Yelling at one another about this or that, over each other and around them. Every time one of them looked pissy, someone would tease them until they were over it. However, to her, it was just loud. This was beyond ridiculous. Putting her fingers in her mouth, she let go of a whistle that stopped them in mid-word. Everyone just stopped and stared at her.

"Who's in charge here?" Everyone, including

the oldest Mr. Strong, pointed to his wife. Jade went to her. "I'm not going to be rude here, or perhaps I am, but I'd like for you to take your family home so that I can get whatever your son wants to say to me over with. I'm tired, unhappy, and well, I'm pissed off."

"At my children?" Jade wouldn't lie to the woman, but she didn't want her to be an enemy either, so she said nothing. "I see. Very closed mouth, are you? Well, I've got a meeting with Mr. Pauly about the new equipment that is coming—" Clay cleared his throat before cutting his mother off.

"It's installed and ready to be used." They all turned to Clay. "I saw her doing it. Pauly was breathing down her neck the entire time that she was working on it too. By the way, Jade designed this particular robot, and I think I can use her help in a great many other projects that I have going on. She's brilliant."

"Is this true?" Again, Jade said nothing, but she did shrug. "We're going to have to work on your communication skills if you're coming to our home for dinner."

"I'm not. Coming to your home for anything,

nor will I be working on my communication skills. I like not having to have a conversation when I don't want to. I've found that it makes people nervous for you not to speak to them, and they confess to all kinds of shit that they think you might have found out. I don't. Find out things, but it is fun for me." Mrs. Strong put her hand on her cheek but didn't say anything. She shocked the woman. Good. "Are you going to take your family home so I can get out of here sooner?"

"I don't think you're going to be as off the hook as you think with this. You saved my son's life, and I owe you." She said that it was her duty as a doctor to make sure that people don't die when she could save them. "Perhaps, but to me, you went beyond what was required of you as a doctor. He was rude to you and mean. Yet you saved him. I can't ever repay you for what you did for us."

When Mrs. Strong stood up, the men did as well. She told them that they were leaving. As soon as she kissed Jenson, she left. One by one, the brothers hugged their brother and wished him luck. The only person that remained behind was Mr. Strong.

"Jenson, don't make me have to come back

here to save your ass, young man." While she had no idea what that meant, Jenson told his father that he'd be on his best behavior. "See that you are."

They were the only two in the room when Jenson's father left. Asking him what he wanted to talk to her about, she sat down in the chair that was as far from the man as she could be without being in another room.

"I wanted to apologize to you for the way I treated you the other day. You had every right to let me lie there and bleed to death, and no one would have blamed you. I owe you my life as well. And I'm profoundly grateful for what you did for me. Despite me being a total ass." She asked him if that was all. "You're very hard on people, aren't you?"

"Not normally, no. Just to jackasses that think that just because I'm waiting tables to pay for my education is beneath them. I accept your apology, Mr. Strong. If there is nothing else, I'd like to get back to work." He asked her if she'd talk to him about her job. "I take orders and fill them when the cook is finished with them."

"I think that is what you think you do, but that's not the job I was talking about. Clay was impressed.

And he doesn't impress easily. What does the robot you designed to do if you don't mind telling me." She said that she didn't but that she did need to get back to work. "I understand. I do. I need to have someone bring me in a computer so that I can get to work too."

Jade stood up, and Jenson asked her if she could come back. Just to talk to him about her job. Confused, she asked him why he was interested in her. When he shrugged and then laughed, she wanted to hit him again.

"I don't have any idea. But talking to you is enjoyable to me. You're hard and brash, and you're fun to be around. Call me a sadist, but I like your show of temper and how you don't have any trouble whatsoever telling me to fuck off when I screw up." She called him an idiot. "I've been called worse. However, I think you might well be right on this. I'm an idiot that wants to tick you off just so you show that lovely temper of yours."

"I'm leaving. On my way out, I'm going to have them do a scan of your head. You're off your rocker." After she left and the nurse came to ask him if he thought he had a concussion, he laughed. Jenson couldn't remember the last time he'd had such a good time pissing another person off. Telling the nurse he was fine, she left him alone. As soon as he was out of here, he was going to find Jade and have some more fun with her.

~*~

Hilda didn't order anything but a glass of water at the restaurant that Jade said she'd meet her at. Not that she expected her daughter to treat her any differently than she ever did, Hilda knew she'd been a terrible mother, but things were different now. She was different. Hilda hoped that her daughter would see that too.

"Mother." Jade was the most beautiful woman that Hilda had ever seen. Even when she was dressed in a large sweatshirt and jeans, she looked like royalty. "I'm starving, so if we could have the conversation at the end, I'd appreciate that. Order whatever you want. I'm paying."

After thanking her, Hilda picked up the menu to hide her tears. It was no less than she deserved. When Jade pushed the menu down, there was no hope for her holding back her tears. Sobbing as quietly as she could—trying hard not to embarrass Jade, she sobbed out her entire troubles.

"I know you said to wait, but I don't know what to do. I'm too old for this. Jade, I never thought that I'd be able to get pregnant at my age." Jade didn't say anything, but if the look on her face was any indication, she was pissed. "Don't be mad at me. Please? I'm having so many thoughts right now that I'm terrified of my own body. What am I do to?"

"I haven't a clue." Jade looked around the restaurant before turning back to her. "I don't want to be nasty or anything, but do you know who the father is?"

She knew what she was saying. On Jade's birth certificate, it said unknown where the space was for a father's name. Nodding, she told her that he'd been her long-time boyfriend until he passed away about a month ago. Jade asked her what he'd died from.

"They said that he had an undetected aneurysm in his brain that killed him. We'd been together for five or so years. His kids were blaming me for his death, but the judge—they took me to court—said that there was no proof at all that I'd done anything wrong. He left me a little money and the house we'd been living in. I can live there forever and not have to worry about anything. Until I found out I was going to have a child. What am I going to do?"

"Are you going to have it?" Hilda told her that she was, but she didn't want to raise it. "Let me think about this. Let's eat, and then we'll figure something out. Just order. We'll eat and discuss your options."

"Thank you, Jade. I'm so sorry to spring this on you like this, but I don't have anyone else to turn to since Charlie passed away." Hilda felt better after talking to her daughter about the baby. When Jade asked her why it had taken her so long to contact her, Hilda felt terrible for saying it out loud. "Because of my age, the doctor was worried that the baby might be, well, he called it unhealthy. Down syndrome was the biggest factor, but he said that Charlie had an inheritable disease that might make the baby not be able to survive past its birth. I guess two of his children had the same thing and only lived a few days. I got the test results back last week and was, I will admit, thrilled to be having a child. But I know now that I couldn't do it. Not even if Charlie were still alive. He was in his fifties, and I was in my forties. It would have been too much on us, and we wouldn't have been able to raise the child well enough between the two of us."

The waiter took their order and then refilled her water, bringing a fresh glass for Jade as well. Not much time passed when they brought their salads. Hers was small in comparison to Jade's. Hilda was surprised every time she had a meal with her daughter at how much she could eat. Yet she remained rail thin and healthy looking.

The doctor had told her that she needed to eat better and rest more if she expected to have a healthy baby and have herself healthy at the end of it. If she rested more than she did now, she'd definitely be a couch potato. But the eating part was difficult for her. All her life, even before she'd had Jade, she'd done fast food. French fries, burgers, and all the pop that she could drink.

After having all her teeth removed, it had been a real eye-opener for her. Not that it stopped her all that much, but she did stop drinking soda and stuck to just water. It was much cheaper, too, when she had to get something to eat on her own.

She had only picked at her salad, not liking all the greens that were in it. But she did eat the cucumbers and tomatoes. When her lunch was sitting in front of her, she looked at the burger and fries like it was something new to her. Looking at Jade when she said something, she asked her if she was all right.

"Yes. It's been a while since I've eaten out. Is this the biggest burger on the menu, or did I mess up and order from like the hungry man side of it?" Jade laughed. Hilda hadn't ever heard her daughter laugh before, and it hurt her in her heart that she'd gotten so far from her daughter that she didn't know she could laugh with such beauty. "I'll have to be more careful in the future when I order, I guess. Not just because of the portion but also how big I might get with this child."

"What do you want to do with the baby? You've already said that you're going to go through the pregnancy, which I think is good. But then what? I know too that you said that you didn't think you were in any position to raise it. However, you must have some idea as to what you're going to do with it."

"It's a boy. They told me that when they did the tests on him." Hilda didn't want to eat now. She was stressing again. But Jade told her they weren't leaving the table until she ate at least half the burger. "To be honest with you, I've not thought beyond knowing that I can't raise it. Talking to you about it helps, but I'm forever stressed out that I might hurt him or something. I'm sorry to admit this to you, but I don't think I was this worried about it when I was having you, Jade."

"You were too young. Everyone said that to you. There is no telling how I might have turned out had you given me up. So we'll just leave that as it is. Done and nothing we can go back and change." Jade finished off her burger and was eating her fries as she continued. She asked her when she was due. After telling her, Jade spoke again. "All right, you have about seven months to decide what sort of adoption you want to go with. I can help you—"

"Will you take him?" Hilda didn't know where that had come from. It had never been in her mind before this. But now that it was out there, she thought it a brilliant idea. But only if her daughter would do it. Otherwise, she'd just give it up. "I know that's a great deal to ask of you. Especially after the way I raised, or I guess sort of raised you. But knowing that he's going to be going to a safe home and with someone that loves him, I'd feel less stressed about everything that is going on right now. Again, I know it's a great deal to ask of you. But will you at least think about it?"

"I don't know, mom. I don't know anything about children." Hilda said because she'd never been a child but only in age. "True. But this, raising a child on my own, even if he is my half-brother, would be something that would require me to make a lot of changes in my life."

"I understand. I do." Jade said that she'd not said no but only thought about the changes. "I won't try and talk you into it. So for now, until you mention it to me, we'll just leave it where it is."

Relieved beyond anything that she'd ever thought of before, Hilda finished her lunch. Not only did she finish off the burger but the dish of ice cream that Jade had ordered for her. While she didn't know what she was going to do in the meantime about the baby, Hilda decided that she was going to do her utmost best to make sure that not only was he healthy but that they both were. Jade and she sat at the table for a long while, just talking about the things they'd been up to since they'd seen each other. Then she talked about the diner that had been closed down.

"You've no idea how much I'm going to miss

that place. For as much as I dislike people in general, I loved the regulars that would come in and say hi to me like we were best of friends." She asked her what had happened. "Ms. B didn't want to run it anymore. And after trying for years to get someone to take it over, she finally just said she was done. Some large companies bought it and the acres surrounding it. I wanted to buy it. But she said that I needed to get out of waiting tables and use my degrees for something other than slinging hash. I think she was right about that. I've been making some progress on some of my designs that I've been putting off."

"Are you financially all right? As I said, Charlie left me a bit of money, and I can help you with bills if you—boy, isn't that a change for us. Me wanting to lend you money. But I'd be glad to help you out." Jade told her that she was doing very well and that she didn't need anything right now. "If you do, you'll let me know, right?"

"I will." She could tell that something was bothering her but didn't pry. One thing that she knew about Jade was that she'd tell you when she was ready and not a moment before. "Have you heard of the Strong family?"

"Yes. They've been around since before I was born. They're said to be extremely wealthy and don't have to work, yet they do. I've heard they come from old money. Why do you ask?" Jade told her of the incident at the diner on her last day. Then she told her about how she'd gone to talk to the older son and that he'd told her that he liked to piss her off. "Well, that's strange. You might want to steer clear of him. He sounds like he's not right in the head."

"That's just what I thought too. Who pisses someone off just to laugh at them?" There was more to it than that, but again, Hilda didn't pry. Thinking about it while Jade told her about his family, she realized that her daughter was intrigued by the man.

As much as she wanted to point out to her that the man had more than likely been flirting with her, she knew better than to say that. Not only would Jade deny it, but she thought that she'd simply move away from him just to avoid any kind of lasting relationship. And if there was anyone in the world that deserved lasting love, it would be Jade. No one, she thought, had loved her since her birth.

Hilda loved her now. But when she'd been a baby, Hilda didn't treat her right. Not only did she ignore her for days on end, but she'd leave her on her own so that she'd not have to be bothered with her. But that didn't last all that long.

Jade did what she needed to do to make sure that they were both safe. Not only that, but bills had been paid on time. There was food in the pantry and soda in the fridge when she wanted it. Then after a while, she noticed that Jade wasn't home as much as she needed her to be. Hilda could only admit this now. She missed her daughter because she had been taking care of her, and there was no one around to clean up after her either. Hilda had used her daughter to the point that she simply left her. Alone and without any way of contacting her.

"Mom? Are you all right? You sort of zoned out there for a moment." She said she'd been thinking about the baby. "Yes, I would guess that he'd be foremost in your mind at all times. I promise that I'll get back to you soon. I need to make sure that I can mentally take care of an infant. I believe that I can, but I want to put all my ducks in a row before I commit to anything. Is that all right with you?"

"Yes, of course, it is. Whatever you need. If you wish to talk to my doctor, then I'll have him call you, or you can call him." Jade hugged her when they were parting, and Hilda had to sit in her car for several minutes before she felt like she could drive home.

Hilda got home in plenty of time for her to take a nap before dinner. She'd been doing that a great deal lately. Even before she'd found out she was going to have a child. Closing her eyes, she thought of Jade raising her child and felt good about it. She didn't have any illusions about it bringing them closer together. She was the one that was in the wrong, and Hilda was just glad that she was willing to meet her for a meal once in a while. It was, she thought, more than she deserved.

The child would be better with his sister than with her. Adopting him out gave her the willies because she was forever reading about how adopted children were treated. She knew that not all homes were like that, but this was her child, and she was going to make sure that, even if she had to keep him, he was in a safe place.

Letting sleep comfort her, Hilda put her hand over her tight belly and thought of her child. He'd be all right. She had to keep telling herself that. Her little boy would be all right.

Chapter 3

Jenson was going to be staying with his parents until he was able to care for himself. Just the ride from the hospital to their home had worn him out to the point that he needed a nap. Then there was the pain in his leg. Taking medications as soon as he could to take the god-awful pain away, he lay on the couch, where he wanted to be, until someone wanted him. He was just waking up when he saw Jade sitting across from him.

"Hello." She said that his mother had called for her to come over and that she'd made her sit in here. "That's all right. I didn't hear anything. Did she tell you why you were to come over?"

"She said that she needed to have someone care for your ass and wanted to know if I could recommend someone. I think she's hoping that I'll take the job. But you won't last a day if I have to pamper you. I don't even know why she thinks I'd give her a good recommendation." Jenson laughed. "You're very odd. Has anyone ever told you that before? You laugh at the strangest things."

"I find you delightful. And beautiful." Her cheeks pinked up, and he smiled then. "Mom told me when I got here that she was going to find someone to make sure that my wounds are healing well. I had no idea that she'd bother you about it."

"No worries. I have no trouble telling people no when I don't want to do something." When she stood up and began pacing, he watched her. Since he had no idea what she would be worrying about, he just let her pace. Moving to a better position on the couch, he felt his body tighten up when she stopped moving. "I had lunch with my mom today. I thought it was going to be an easy meal. I'd turn her down about money, and I'd be on my way. However, nothing is as easy as you hope it might be, is it?"

"No generally, no. Is she all right?" Jade began

pacing again. "I didn't know you had anything to do with your mom. I mean, you've been at the diner since you were just a kid, right?"

"Mom had to grow up, and I wasn't going to be her sitter anymore." She continued to pace, and he wondered if she realized just how beautiful she was. "She told me that she's going to have a baby."

Now that floored him. While not knowing how old her mother was, he thought that since Jade was in her early twenties, her mother would be at the very least twenty or so years older than her. He asked if she was all right with that.

"No. She's not. And for the record, my mom is only just forty. She had me just after her sixteenth birthday. But that's not the point. She wants me to take the baby and raise it. She didn't say that I would be his mom or sister, but she wants me to raise him so that she can make sure that he's safe." Again, about a million questions were going through his head, but he didn't voice them. One of them did she make sure that she had been safe. "I know nothing about babies. Less about having a brother. I'm sure you have all kinds of information on that with having five brothers, but I have nothing to reference it with."

"I can tell you whatever you want to know. However, there are only a few years between all of us. There will be at least twenty-five years between the two of you." She nodded but didn't stop pacing. When his mom came into the room, she asked if there was a problem.

"I'm not sure that I can share this with you. It's her family." Jade continued to pace, and he smiled at his mom. "It's not me this time, so I'm all right. However, if you'd not mind finding me a physician, I think that I might have pulled out a couple of stitches when I sat up."

"Let me look." Jade helped him to sit up on the couch without making him hurt more. He noticed, too, that she was strong. Mom sent dad out to Jade's car to get her medical bag, and while he was doing that, Jade cut away the bandage. The site of his blood had him laying his head back on the couch and not looking. "You did break a couple of the stitches. I can put them back if you want. I have something to numb the area but nothing to knock you out. What do you want to do? Or, you might want to go to the emergency room to get it done."

"You do it. Please." She said that she would

and set to work. Again, she told him everything that she was doing for him. Jenson didn't feel the needle enter his leg when she was numbing him, but when she pulled at the stitches that she had to cut around, he was sick at that feeling. "Is it looking all right?"

"Yes. No infection that I can see. Your skin is cool to the touch." He didn't look but listened to her voice. It was calming. "All right. I'm going to put in about ten stitches. I'm making mine smaller because they tend to last a bit longer. When you can sit in a shower, I'd make sure that you keep this area clean and then dry when you're finished."

"How soon can I get up and around?" She said that his physician would be able to tell him that. But she'd not make any plans for the next week anyway. "Good. The pain is only bad enough that I need drugs for it when I move around. I'm sick of sitting on my ass all day and not doing anything."

"You could get yourself a wheelchair. With your upper body strength, you could get yourself around more. Just take it easy. Even if you wanted to go outside for a little while would be good. Blow the stink of being hurt off of you. It'll also clear your mind." Mom said that she'd get him one so that he could get around. "If you call the medical department at the hospital, they can get him set up with the things that he'll need to shower himself too. A sit-down one, but it'll feel good to have your body washed up, and hair washed."

Mom left them to take care of that for him. When he felt the bandage wrapped around his leg again, he was able to raise his head. There was no one in the room with them, and he watched her as she finished up with his leg.

Her hair was dark and long. She'd pulled it up in a bun at some point, and little wisps of it were curling down around her face. Every time she blew it out of her eyes, he wanted to push it back out of her way just so he could see if it was as soft as it looked. Her eyes were dark too. But not brown like his were, but blue. Almost black looking.

She had the most flawless skin. Dimples when she smiled and tiny freckles across the bridge of her nose. When she licked her lips, he groaned. Then he cried out in pain when she pinched him. At least she did it on the other leg.

"Ouch. What was that for?" She stood up so quickly that he nearly dropped his leg to the floor. "I didn't do anything to you."

"You were looking at me like I was a chicken pot pie." Jenson couldn't help it. He burst out laughing. "You're insane. Why would you think that was funny? I'm leaving here before I get blamed for you being stupid."

"No. Please don't leave. I'm sorry. I truly am. But I was thinking of you like a nice juicy steak. Why chicken pot pie?" She told him it was her favorite comfort food. And that she didn't care for steaks at all. "Yes, I love them for that as well. With cornbread on the side and it dumped over a pile of mashed potatoes."

"Ms. B would make that for me for every birthday. The cornbread too. Once I had it dumped over the taters, I would crumble up my cornbread for that added extra flavor." His belly growled this time, and he heard hers do the same. "I have to get going. I have three more things I have to do on the way back to my place, and I don't have time to be hanging out with you."

"Oh, I thought you were staying for dinner." His mom kissed him on the cheek when she sat down beside him, smiling at Jade. "Please stay for dinner with us. While I have an idea that it's going to be all of Jenson's favorites, perhaps you can find something you'll enjoy too. We're having potato cheese soup with homemade bread. There will be sandwiches too. I think anyway. Also, for dessert, bread pudding with cranberries in it with a dark caramel sauce."

"I shouldn't." Jenson could tell that she was on the verge of staying when he told her that she could have anything she wished so long as the cook had the ingredients. "All right, but no hanky panky shit. I've enough on my plate right now without having to hurt you again for my virginity." The glare that Jade gave him nearly had him laughing again.

However, he held it back. His mom looked as confused as he'd ever seen her, but Jenson was all right with that too. This woman would, if he wanted to pursue her, keep him on his toes for the rest of his day. And Jenson decided that he wanted to see this paragon of a woman as often as she'd allow it. He'd have to be on his best behavior, or he'd miss out on something great.

The wheelchair had arrived shortly before dinner. And dinner was held until he was able to maneuver the wheelchair around the house. His leg was braced up and strapped in. Lucky for him, too, that the rest was longer than his leg, or he might have bumped it several times. As it was, he was able to eat in the dining room with his family and Jade. Clay joined them just as pudding was being served and talked to Jade about the equipment that had shown up at his house.

"The tiny drill is wonderful for getting into smaller places. And it's powerful too. I have so many uses for it now that I can't wait to get together with my team to see what we can do with it." Jade told him that she had a smaller one that she was working on that helped her with working on the robotics. "That's fantastic. I mean, really. Why aren't you working for NASA or some other government agency building tools for us to use?"

"They decided that they couldn't afford me. But they do call up when they think they need something." Clay said they needed to get their heads out of their collective asses and off their back pockets. The government needed her innovation. "To work for them full time, I'd need the difference to work on the other projects I enjoy more. I've two such things now that are going to be used for getting people in and out of bed easier. Also, a way for their sheets or clothing to be changed without heavy lifting on anyone's part. Nurses are overworked enough as it is, so this helps them out." Jenson asked if she'd been contacted by someone or just noticed the need. "Both, I guess. My cousin, Holly, her brother-in-law is a nurse, and he hurt his back a few years back by trying to lift someone out of their bed. I'm not finished with it just yet, but Robert helps me out by coming by to use it when I tweak something else. I love doing things like this." Jenson was impressed.

The rest of the meal was talking about what sort of things everyone was involved in. Jenson was running for congress in the next voting, and he was telling her that she was doing things that were on his campaign platform.

"You should talk to some of the elders at the nursing homes about things that have been fucked around with for the people in their age group. Most of them end up in the hospital when their family has had enough of them. Or they want to run off for a few days without them. They need to have a place where they can go to hang out with younger people. Not a huge campaign platform by any means, but I was caught up in one of their lives a few days ago when I was reinstalling a monitor in the emergency department." He asked her what had happened that she ended up there. "Her family found out that she was leaving her money to a charity and not to them, and they stuck her in the hospital until someone else found a place for her to go. More than likely a nursing home. It happens a great deal."

"I'm sure that it does. My grandma worked right up until she died." Jenson listened while Clay talked about their grandparents. "Granddad retired from his job and had nothing to do but get under Grandma's feet, he told me. He might well have lived a good deal longer had he had something to do or people to hang out with. But the money, our money, was and still is a barrier for people to want to get close to us. I'm sure you have the same issues."

"I don't have any friends because I'm caustic. It has nothing to do with how much is in my bank account." They all laughed, including Jade. "I know that I'm considered wealthy, but I don't think of myself as anything but the woman who waited tables for a living for what seems like longer than I've been alive. I have a roof over my head. Not one that I liked, but it was all I could find when the diner closed. I have a car that is almost as old as I am that I keep running on my own. Food in the pantry even though I would rather go out and have someone wait on me. I can cook, thanks to Ms. B, but it's not something that I want to do every day. I have a great education, health and life insurance, and a company that I built up from nothing. I'm proud of myself in that area. However, I don't have anyone that I can call up and ask for help. Nor do I make friends easily. I have a lot of people that are acquaintances but no one that I'd depend on. Not because of them, but I just don't trust a great many people."

"That's sad," Jade told him that it is what it is. "No. I think that you could easily change that if you wish. Make friends and have some fun outside of work. It could be your upbringing that has you not trusting anyone. However, I don't know your family, only the little that you told me, so I have no frame of reference. I like you. Yes, you are a little caustic, but I find that to be somewhat funny."

"Because you're weird." Jenson laughed. As they retired to the living room, he was shown how to get out of the wheelchair and onto the couch. He'd be able to go to the bathroom the same way as mom had ordered him a toilet set as well as something he would be able to shower too. The thought of a shower made him giddy. It had been a week since he'd been able to feel like he was clean.

Jade left not too long after he was on the couch. There was no persuading her to stay longer, and he felt her gone all the way to his toes. Mom and dad went to pick up a few of his clothes from his home, and Clay sat across from him on the couch. He looked serious.

"I asked her out. Did you know that?" Hurt but not sure why he asked his brother what she'd said. "No. Just that. No. You like her, don't you?"

"I don't know what I feel about her, to be honest. I love to see her angry, which, as she's pointed out to me several times, is weird. I like talking to her as well. She's not out to impress anyone. Nor is she intimidated by how much money we have. Jade is woefully unimpressed by me altogether. To be honest, I'm not sure how I feel about that. I've never had to go so far out of my way to impress a woman before."

"I can see that." Clay stretched out his legs and

was quiet for a few moments. "I won't ask her out again until you make it clear that you're not going to date her. However, I will tell you this, Jenson. You hurt her in any way again, and I won't stop hurting you ten times as bad. She's a nice person. A little on the cautious side, I will say that, but she's a great person. I like being around her too."

"I've come to realize that I did hurt her by my words and actions. I don't blame her for knocking me on my ass. I deserved it. The very fact that she is still coming around makes me think that she isn't one to hold a grudge. I like her, Clay. I don't know why but I do. Thank you for telling me your feelings." Clay shrugged. "I'm going to share with you what she told me tonight. Her mom is going to have a baby. A little boy. She wants Jade to raise him. Since she told me that, all I can think about is Jade heavy with my child. Does that make any sense to you? I mean, we barely know each other, and she seems to not like me at all. Yet I want to see her having my child. Our child."

"If you get together, and I'm not sure how that will work out for you, but if the two of you were to come together and she does take her brother as her child, how will you feel about him?" He thought his brother had a good question and the first thought in his head was to tell him that it wouldn't make a bit of difference to him so long as she loved him. "You want her to fall in love with you? Jenson, I don't know if you realize this or not, but I think that you're about as in love with a woman you've only just met as our parents are with one another."

~*~

Watching the printer do its job, Jade felt her mind pinging off on about thirty different things. It was getting more and more difficult for her to concentrate on any one thing without her mind drifting off to other territories at once. Two things in particular that were taking up the room were her mom and Jenson.

She'd gone to see her mother's doctor after she'd okayed it to have her talk to him. Everything that she'd told her was correct. The baby was healthy and a boy. Mom did need to eat better, and he said that she'd been given a diet plan to follow. Mom's due date was in early May. Since it was now November, there were only six months for her to make her decision on whether or not to adopt the little boy.

Every time she thought of raising her brother, her mind immediately flipped to Jenson. Like he was simply going to be a part of their lives. She didn't understand that at all. The man was certifiable, and she didn't particularly care for him all that much.

His mother had been keeping her updated on his care. Why she was doing that wasn't making any sense in her mind, much like anything else concerning the man, but she thanked her politely each time she called, or worse yet, when she came by her new office building.

"How long have you been in here? It looks like you've been here for ages." She told Mrs. Strong just yesterday that she'd been waiting on the finalization of the sale and had marked out where she wanted each piece to go. That she'd only been in the building for a few days. "I guess being an engineer, you'd be able to have precise measurements. When we bought a summer home a while back, I had the movers moving things around until they fit in the room. Even then, I had to get rid of some of the pieces that I thought would fit. How are you doing?"

"Great. I'm working, and that's all I can hope for. Why are you here?" Mrs. Strong insisted that she call her by her given name, but she wouldn't do that. It would, she told her imply that they were more than acquaintances. "We're not, you know. I mean, I'm not being rude, but I don't understand what it is you want or need from me."

"I don't need anything, Jade. I just enjoy being with you. I have, as you know, so many males in my family that it's seldom that I get to enjoy a nice conversation with a female. Even if you're slightly rude." Jade had felt her face heat up, and that made her a little defensive. But before she could lash out, the older woman laughed. "It's nothing to do with anything other than you're easy to talk to. You don't seem to have any feelings of being beneath me. Where that term came from has always irked me. No one is beneath anyone if you ask me. Now, how about we go and have some lunch together? Just the two of us hanging out together."

"Are you just trying to be a friend to me? Not that I'd understand why you'd want to do that, but I'm not sure how this would work. Also, you should know that your sons have been by to ask me out. I'm not dating them, just so you know." She asked her why not. "Why not? I'm not really into dating anyone in the first place. Secondly…well, I'm not going to raise the beneath you issue up, but really, they should be dating debs or even someone much more in line with, I don't know, your kind of people."

"My kind—what on earth does that mean?" Jade didn't have an answer, but Mrs. Strong thought it was funny. "Dear child, my boys are grown men, and if they want to date someone, then I'm all for them having a good time. If they fall in love, then whomever the woman is, I hope that she'll accept me into their lives as much as they can. I'm not a snob, young lady. Which one of them is starting to wear you down? Let me think. Clay. He's the most persistent of all of my sons. And you have so much in common. Perhaps that's—"

"Jenson. He calls me every day to talk to me. Even when I tell him to stop. If I can't come to the phone for some reason, then he sends someone by. Yesterday he sent me a cell phone so that I'd be able to talk to him when I wanted. I don't want to." Her face heated again. This conversation with his mother was awkward and making her a little defensive. "He's driving me insane."

"Insane, or is it something else? I won't tell him

if you want to talk about it. I promise you, Jade, that whatever you tell me, unless it will cause either of you harms, I will not divulge a secret." She didn't tell her anything. At least nothing until they were seated at one of the few restaurants in town that did a good lunch. "I love this place. Bar and I come here a couple of times a month for dinner and their fried pies. My favorite is lemon, and his is peach. But I'll eat any or all of them if given the chance. Now, tell me what is bothering you. It is, I can tell."

After telling her about her mother, she asked if she'd come to any decisions. Telling her no, she'd not, Jade then moved on to a problem that she was having with the hospital. Not talking about Jenson if she could avoid it.

"I'm on the hospital board. Let me look into what you're saying about Pauly. He's been a burr up my bottom for some time now." Jade asked her why she believed her. "I have no reason not to believe you. And his not having the billing paid is something that I've heard rumors about from him before. No one has come forward as you have about it, so now I can take care of it. The man is a nuisance if you ask me."

"I'm not hurting for the money, at least at the

moment. I've paid my employees for their work on it but come next month, I'm going to have to dip into my accounts to make payroll and billings. It's a substantial amount of money. Not just for the equipment but the installation as well as the yearly amount for us to come in and service the equipment that we installed last year. I don't want anyone hurt when a piece of my equipment becomes broken, but I can't afford to keep putting money into a pit that has no intentions of paying for the service."

"I'm thinking that this is more than a few thousand dollars, isn't it?" She nodded. "I see. How much are we talking total that the hospital is behind with you? Just a ballpark if you don't know precisely how much."

"Just over four million dollars. Plus late fees. I've billed the hospital for the last equipment and installation, but they have forty-five days to pay that. That's another million and change." Mrs. Strong whistled. "I've tried to get an attorney to take them on, but since it's a not-for-profit hospital, I'm having difficulties getting even that part done."

"The hospital isn't a not-for-profit one. Who told you that? Let me guess, Pauly." She nodded. "The little bastard. Let me call Jenson. He's an attorney. I think that for you, he'd take that on. Just so he thinks that he's being able to repay a little of what he thinks he owes you."

That had been yesterday and today, not only did she have an appointment with Jenson at his parent's home, but she had had to gather up all the contracts with the hospital that she'd gotten and sent them over to him. Since she was good at keeping everything that she signed, it was just a matter of pulling the file.

Driving her car over to the house, when she realized that she wasn't getting shit done at the office, she was surprised to see that not only were Jenson and his parents there but so were all his brothers. When she asked what was going on, a little afraid of the group of them altogether, she was asked to sit down.

"I've had my brothers go to the hospital to make sure that each of the pieces of equipment that you have invoices for is installed. This isn't on you, but Pauly is claiming that you've not only lied about the equipment, but the prices that you're trying to get out of this are triple what the estimate is. By the way, great job on keeping records of not just the estimates and invoices. Also, the times that you called as well as a note on what was said. That is going to be so helpful." She asked him if she was going to get her money. "Yes. I've also gone ahead on your behalf and gotten the money for your latest install and equipment."

He handed her an envelope. There were five checks. It paid off each of the four invoices that she'd been sending to the hospital. The last check was, Jenson told her, for late fees as well as time and aggravation.

"I didn't expect this so quickly. How did you do this when I've been threatening him for a year or so." Jenson told her. "Oh. I guess I never thought of him being fired for this. I can see that it's a good reason, but it never—did you take your fees out of this money?"

As if they'd heard some secret sound, the entire family got up and left her and Jenson in the room alone. When she started to rise to leave, he asked her to please have a seat. She did, but she was ready to leave if he said something snarky to her.

"I would like to ask you out on a date. No

strings attached to the money. That's why I gave it to you first. I just want to see you on a personal level. You're all I've thought about for the last week and a half." She asked him why. "Why what? I'm not sure that I understand. Why do I want to see you? You're an amazing woman. You make me laugh. Mostly at myself, but I like that too. For all I know, this could just be nothing, but I can't stop thinking about you and being a part of your life. Even the thought of you walking out the door right now makes me feel like I'm going to be missing something great. Please, Jade. Will you just have dinner with me tomorrow night, and we can see where it goes from there?"

Chapter 4

Herbert hadn't even been able to empty his desk when the police showed up to escort him out of the hospital. Whoever had a burr up their ass about him had better be watching themselves. He was going to find out who they were and make sure they knew that he was in charge no matter who it was they sat at his desk. They'd not even used the security team at the hospital, but real cops had come in with their hands on their weapons while he'd been having lunch and took him out in cuffs. And in front of everyone in the dining room.

"Damn it all to hell and back. What is going to happen now that I'm not there?" Not that he thought that he had made much of a difference at the hospital. He was more of a putting his hand out and getting money than a handshaking person who got things done. Herbert had been responsible for the hospital having the funding to build a new ward for the city, but no one brought that up when he was asked why he was being fired.

He did think that the Anderson woman had had something to do with it, but she was simply too stupid to find herself an attorney, much less have had the paperwork that he'd been fobbing her off with. It had been a thrill for him to know that he'd not paid a single bill that she sent to the office every few weeks.

"That's the way that you saved money. You wouldn't pay anything, and eventually, they'd have to give up, knowing that it was a lost cause." He didn't like talking to himself, but he also didn't want his mom to be privy to what he had been up to. As far as she knew, he was working in a pizza place every day and barely had enough money to keep the cable on for her. It was, he supposed, her home that he was living in for free. And the bills were being paid out of her money. However, she was as dumb as a rock. Since his father had died a few years ago, he'd been 'taking care of her.' Sometimes he'd forget that she was even in the house unless someone asked about her. The staff, her staff, would care for her, even going to her with questions of the household instead of him. Herbert supposed that was all right. Not being bothered by anything at home was all right with him.

"Mr. Pauly, your mother would like a word with you." He asked the butler what she wanted now. "She would like a word with you, sir."

He had to find her. And that pissed him off. Finding her in the library sitting at the desk that he'd taken for himself when he moved into the house aggravated him even more. Not bothering with sitting, he knew the chairs in this room were set so that whoever sat in them was lower than the person at the desk. He stood by the fireplace, making himself look bored.

"I've had a phone call from a Mrs. Lisa Strong. You know who she is, correct?" He said that he did. Then asked her what she wanted. "I want a great many things, Herbert, but the things that I've set in motion in the last two hours are going to give me the greatest pleasure."

"What are you going on about? I have to return to work soon, and you're keeping me from being on time. I know how you think punctuality is so important." She said that everyone should. "I don't care. What did the old bat want with you? Is she out of money?"

"Doubtful that any of them will ever run out of money. And they all work outside of the home, too, making a living rather than sucking the bank dry. Also, I've known for some time that you don't work at a pizza place, as you have told me numerous times. I also know that you've been fired as head of the hospital today for mishandling of funds. What do you have to say about that?" Herbert said that he'd get his job back. And that she'd help him. "Help you? No, I'm afraid that isn't going to happen. I've been helping the Strongs, Jenson, as a matter of fact, with having you brought to your knees. I'm finished with you, Herbert, and as of now, you're no longer living here. The staff has packed up your suits and undies and put them in a box for you. They'll be waiting for you too –"

"What are you talking about? There had better not be one thing out of place in my room, mother or I'm going to be pissed off more than I am now." She just snorted at him. Like she was something of a commoner. He pointed that out to her. "You're nothing like my grandmother in being rich. She knew how to treat underlings when they came sniffing her out for money. You just hand it over and have a beer with the person. If you keep this up, there will be nothing left for me. You're a disgrace to the name Pauly."

"Oh, but there is nothing left to you, son. Not one red cent. The things that your grandmother that you loved so much left to you aren't any longer yours to claim, not that you would have ever been able to pay the thing that was in arrears in your lifetime. What happened to her home, you might ask. I know. You pilfered it away until the state took it for nonpayment of taxes. Good thing that I had a spy on that one. I own it now. Along with the things that you never took care of with her will." He said the estate was to pay the taxes, so he'd not have to worry about it. "If there had been an estate left when you moved into the house, that is true. But as I said, you spent all the money that was there for such things as taxes and repairs that should have lasted a lifetime for you."

"I was waiting on you to die so that I could pay them. Not that it matters now. With you taking them as your own, I'll get them when you are dead. Not soon enough for me." She laughed at him. "Why are you thinking that this is funny? I can, but you're going to be shit out of luck when I rule the household. Why you ever made me get a job in the first place is beyond me. There's always been enough money for us not to have to work. Yet you did. All the time. Why? Because it made you special? It didn't, let me tell you that. You're nothing to me. I loathe you."

"I'm so glad to hear you say that, Herbert." When she gave a little nod, three men seemed to just appear in the room. They hadn't, of course. They'd been standing there the whole time. But since they weren't important to him and this conversation, he ignored them. "This is my new attorney, Jenson Strong. Also, to his left is an IRS agent, Agent Ryan Quarter. The other person is the new head of the hospital board, Mr. Bar Strong, Jenson's father."

"So? What does that have to do with you trying to kick me out? Nothing." He looked at the three men and saw that one of them was on crutches. Jenson was disabled, and his mother was still going to hire him? Not over his dead body. "Go away, all of you. My mother and I are discussing where she's going to end up when I get a doctor to sign off on her being addled all the time." When his mother laughed, Herbert looked at the doorway when another man walked into the room. His name, he told him, was Howard Ferry.

"I'm a certified physician, and I have examined your mother and found that she is of sound mind. Also, she is in remarkable shape. Could be from her working instead of sitting behind a desk all the time." He laughed and then asked Herbert if he wanted a copy of the exam results. He declined. "With this examination, the changes that she made to her will are validated and not found to be done under duress nor threat of harm."

"Changes to her will? What's that supposed to mean? What changes have you made, mother? You'd better not be cutting me out of the shit I have coming to me." There was a great deal of laughter going on, and he was fucking sick of it. "Mother? What trouble have you caused me that I'm going to have to fix?"

"You are no longer in my will, Herbert. I have,

and I'm so proud of this, made Jenson executor of my estate when I die, and he'll carry out my wishes to the letter. The reasons that I could list as to why I've taken you out are too numerous to list right now but rest assured, Jenson has the list that I've been keeping about you. Also, I'm going to keep adding to the list as you screw up."

"This is ridiculous. Where is all *my* money going?" She told him that it was none of his business. "That is where you're wrong, mother dear. It's going to be my money when you finally are dead, and I won't have you giving it away to every Tom, Dick, and Harry with their hands out."

"Like you have been doing all your life. You even stole from the hospital where I thought you'd be doing good things. However, that's finished as well. As is our mother-son relationship. I want nothing more to do with you, Herbert. You've done nothing but shame me since you were out of kindergarten. I'm ashamed to say this, but while I do love you, I don't like you one bit." He told her that he hated her and had never loved her. "Well, I guess it's a good thing that I've taken steps to have you out of my life. Agent Quarter, he's all yours."

"Mr. Pauly, I'm here to arrest you on tax evasion." He just stared at the man. "The money that you have stored in the bank's safety deposit box has been confiscated. As well as the other checking account that you had stashed money in."

"No. You can't touch that. It says right on my checks that it's my account. You can't touch *my* money." He was handcuffed and told his rights. "What are you doing? Mother, you have to do something. This isn't right. That is the money that I took fair and square."

"You're an idiot." He glared at Jenson. "Did you think that by simply putting that it was your account that no one would bother with it? Putting the safety deposit box number on the checks was very helpful, too, by the way."

"What does this mean for me getting my money back to me? You've no right in taking what doesn't belong to you." Jenson just shook his head and said nothing. "Well? You're a fool if you think that I'm going to allow this to happen to me. I had to work very hard in making myself a little nest egg for my later years. With my mother's money, I would have been set forever."

"I guess that it sucks to be you since you're getting none of the money." As he was being taken out of the house, he was screaming at his mother to do something. All she did was wave goodbye to him and tell him to have a nice time in prison.

"What the hell are you talking about? No one had a nice time in prison. And you'd better be doing something to keep me from going there." She only waved at him again and closed the door in his face. "Damn it, mother. What is wrong with you?"

He was put in the back of a dark van that had not a single window other than the front ones. As soon as he was seated and buckled in so he'd not fall over, two armed men got in with him. Herbert didn't bother asking them where they were taking him. It didn't matter as he was going to be out as soon as his mother got her head out of her ass and came for him. She'd miss him sooner or later. Then she'd be getting him back home.

~*~

Jenson fussed with his tie three times before he just gave up. When his butler, Samuel Jenkins, helped him out, he could tell that the older man had something on his mind. Asking him about it, the man grinned before telling him what he'd done.

"I did speak to Ms. Jade about the change of venue, sir. She said that she'd be ready in plenty of time. She was, justifiably so, concerned about the implications of her going with you to this dinner. She said that she hoped that once people started to gather around you, you'd explain to them that you were only friends." Samuel had Jenson's tie fixed in seconds. But didn't move. "May I ask what your intentions are for the young lady? I know that it's none of my business, sir, but she is a lovely woman if not a bit…well, on the vocal side."

"I will agree with you on that." Jenson laughed. "I don't know what my intentions for Jade are. Not yet, at any rate. I like her. A great deal. She's not the least bit intimidated by me or my money. Jade keeps me on my toes. When I was finished up this morning with having Pauly arrested, the first person I wanted to talk to was her. She told me to get my ass out of my head and think of it as if I'd done a good thing for a great many people, then she hung up on me. I laughed for a good hour."

"When she called here after I had spoken to her, she asked me what sort of tarty outfit she would be required to wear. I was taken aback if you want to know the truth. But I told her it was a black tie, and she went on about how she didn't own a black tie. I believed that she was serious, but she only told me to 'cool my jets' and that she was joking. If she does become a part of your life, then we'll need to get used to her." Jenson said he would as well, then asked him what he'd told her about black tie dinners. "Nothing. She said she'd look it up. But not to be surprised if she wore sweats and a pair of old socks. You don't think she will, do you, sir?"

"I'm not putting any kind of bets on what she wears. She'll be beautiful even if she wears what she threatened you with." Once he was finished getting dressed with help from Samuel with his shoes, he picked up his cane and walked to the door. "Thank you for getting with my other doctor about using a cane tonight, Samuel. I think if I had shown up in a wheelchair, no one would see me fit to be a congressman."

"I believe, as you said about Ms. Jade, they'd think you the perfect man for the job no matter how you were received. But I don't think she's all that happy with you just using a cane this evening. She said that you were playing with fire and that she'd be prepared for you being in a great deal of pain." Thanking his old friend after telling him that he'd be just fine, Jenson used the elevator to put him on the main level of the house and now worn him out. The limo was parked out in front of the house, and he could see that his parents were already in it, waiting.

This dinner was a huge event, and he was both looking forward to it and not. It was to help pay for his political ambitions. Even though he could well afford it himself, he'd been told that he wasn't to use his own money for such a venture. It would be considered a contribution if he were to do that. And there were a great many people out there that would back him in the form of money. While he could understand that, Jenson was worried that no one would be at the dinner to help him out.

"You're not still thinking that no one will show, are you, son?" He said that it had crossed his mind a few times. "Well, let it go. I know for a fact that every plate was sold to this thing, and donations are coming in very quickly. You're going to be just fine."

"Thanks, Dad. I'm so happy that you guys are behind me on this too. All of you." His mom asked him what Jade thought of going with him. "I've not had a chance to speak to her other than when she hung up on me this morning. She did call the house and asked what she was to wear. She told Samuel that she was wearing sweats and old socks."

They all three laughed. His mom leaned back in her seat and told him not to be flustered when the people there speculated about the woman he was with. Jenson told her that Samuel had warned him of the same thing.

"They'll want to know everything about her. Not just who she is but what sort of relationship the two of you have. Even if you don't comment on the questions, they'll simply make up whatever they wish. It's doubtful to me that Jade would care, but you'll have to keep your cool with what they say or ask of you, or they'll have you married with children in no time." He thought about that but didn't comment to his parents. But his mother seemed to understand. "You're falling in love with her, aren't you, Jenson?"

"I don't know what I feel about her. We've only been in the same room a handful of times. I've spoken to her daily. She's usually berating me about one thing or another and pushing me away. I just keep pushing back to her." His dad asked him if he thought that was all it was. She wasn't impressed by him. "No. I've thought of that. You know, she doesn't want me, so I have to make her kind of thing? But it's more than that. It's like I need her in my life. That sounds dumb, doesn't it?"

"Not at all. Perhaps she'll be just what you need. I have noticed that you're happier since she's been around you. Even Barton has commented on how much he's been enjoying this new you." He asked if he'd been that bad. "I'm your mother, so I can be honest. Yes, you have been a bear to be around before Jade. Snipping and snapping at people. Your staff was afraid to say a word to you about anything for fear of being fired. I do hope that you put a little something in their paychecks to make them realize that you were not raised like that."

"I'll do that. I promise. I knew that I was being a bastard to everyone, but I just couldn't stop. Like I was on this path of ruination or something like that." They pulled up in front of Jade's home, and he knew now why she'd warned him about not getting out of the car, that she'd come out to him. "She's going to have to find a better place to live. This place is dangerous."

"I agree." When dad got out of the car to go to her door, Jenson found himself tensing up for reasons that he didn't understand. As soon as the door opened, dad stepped in, and the door closed again. It was a good five minutes before they both came out of the house and down the stairs to the car. Dad did not look happy.

As soon as they were settled again, with Jade at his side, he asked what had happened. Dad told him he'd talk to him later. However, Jade didn't have such qualms about telling him.

"Your dad is upset that I was robbed this afternoon. The police are still in there looking around. I didn't have anything here yet, for which I'm glad, but your dad seems to think that I should have called one of you to be there for me." Jade looked at his father before continuing. "I'm a big girl, Mr. Strong. And well capable of taking care of myself. I'm just happy that I wasn't home, or I might not have been able to get dressed up for this thing."

"Are you all right?" Jade glared at him and told him that she'd just told him she wasn't home.

"I know, but something like being robbed can be hard on a person. I know that the one time that I was robbed at college, I felt violated for weeks after. All they did was take things from my car after busting the window in."

"I, for one, am glad that you are well. However, since you're going to be with Jenson for the rest of the evening, hanging on his arm, so to speak, I think you should call us by our given names. If only for the press. You were told they'd be there, correct?" She said that Samuel had told her. "Good. Now, my name is Lisa. My husband's name is Barkley, but he is called Bar. And you know Jenson's name. I think you calling him Mr. Strong is going to be talked about, sounding like he'd picked you out of a lineup or something. Also, darling. Don't answer any questions you don't wish to. However, when you do answer them, please be nice. Not that I won't be tempted to blast the press too, but we're here to get funding for Jenson for his seat in congress."

"I do know how to conduct myself, Mrs. Strong. I'm not going to embarrass any of — "

"Oh, my child, I didn't mean...I guess it did sound like I was telling you that you would embarrass us. I'm sorry about that. I was thinking that I'd hate to have you plastered all over the newspapers as a bitch. I'm sure that anything you say will be harmful to you, and I just wanted to warn you how vicious some newspaper people are. I'm profoundly sorry for that." Jade said that she was as well. "You know what? You just be yourself. That's the person that we all like, and if that doesn't make them sit back and take stock on themselves, then we'll just leave."

"I like you, Lisa. You're a quiet ball buster. I do not doubt that you know just how to put people in their place without raising your voice. Yes, I'll have it myself. And I'll make sure that no one is the wiser about how much I hate people." As soon as they pulled up in front of the governor's home, Dad and mom got out of the limo, and he looked at Jade. "Do I have lipstick on my teeth?"

"No. But I'd enjoy kissing what you have on your beautiful lips off." She stared at him. "I don't know if you realize this or not, but I'm falling for you. In a big way."

"Why? Why would you tell me that before I'm going to go into a room full of strangers? How am I supposed to engage with people thinking about what you just said?" He kissed her quickly on the mouth, and she glared. "You're going to be in big trouble if I fall in love with you, Jenson. I'm not easy, and I don't expect you to try anything while I'm out with you. I'm not ready for that."

"I'm not sure that I'm ready for that next step either if you mean making love." She said that was it exactly. "As for you falling in love with me, I couldn't be a happier man if you were. I'm honestly about half in love with you now too."

She didn't move, and he watched her face. There was some emotion there, but she was not giving him any clue as to what she might be thinking. Instead of talking, more than likely making her nervous, he suggested that they join his parents. When she was handed out by his father, Jenson got out next. With his cane on his left side and Jade on his right, Jenson had never felt more complete than he did at this moment.

There were hundreds of people at this dinner. More than he thought that had been invited. When a couple came toward him as soon as they were through the front doors, Jade whispered who they were to him. Being able to greet them as if he knew them was something that he'd not counted on when he'd asked Jade to come with him.

"Mr. and Mrs. Daniels is the next couple coming toward you. He is on the board at the hospital as well." Throughout the predinner gathering, she would tell him the names of people as well as a little tidbit about them that he'd not known. When Mr. and Doctor Burley shook his hand, he knew that they were struggling mentally because their oldest son had been in and out of rehab for the last year. "They could use a little of your campaign about what you're planning, if anything, about a rehab facility."

"Hello, Mr. Burley. Doctor Burley. I'm so sorry to hear about your son. If there is anything that you need, please don't hesitate to call my office." They smiled, but he could tell they were hurt by their son's drug addiction. "I have in the works a plan for getting funding for a facility for the parents or significant others to come and have someone to talk to. I believe that just having a place to go while dealing with this will keep the parents healthy as well. If you want to talk to me or even have a few suggestions on things that you think would be helpful to parents, again, please don't hesitate to call me."

At eight, he was ready to sleep. His leg was bothering him from standing for so long, and he wanted something to eat. Being too nervous before to think about food, he was starving now. Jade, as if she read his mind, handed him a small bottle of water that was ice cold as well as some medication to take. After he took them, thanking her for them, she handed him a small plate of California rolls so he'd make it to dinner. That was when he got a look at what she was wearing.

"Holy Christ, you're beautiful." He might have been just a little loud, and she hushed him. "Honey, you look amazing. I love your dress."

It was a black sheath of silk. It sounded so lame in his mind to call it that but just looking at the way that it clung to her body made him what to find a dark, quiet room to explore the bits of her that were covered up. It was all he could do not to pull her out to the limo and take her back to his home.

Dinner was extravagant. Jenson supposed that paying two hundred dollars a plate would have to be something special. Jade was seated next to him, and his parents were across from the two of them. The table was narrow enough that he could speak to them easily and Jade as well. Making very little small talk while the food was eaten was fine with him. He was not only having a better time than he thought he would, but Jenson was also feeling good about life in general.

However, he was in a great deal of pain. While the medicine he'd taken earlier had taken the worst of it away, he was feeling the effects of being up on his feet for too long. Jade reached for his leg under the table and began massaging the muscle above the wound. Thanking her for everything, he found himself wanting to lean into her shoulder and cry. He was in entirely too much pain for him to think of it as being sexual.

After dinner, Jade made him sit down for the rest of the night. She never left his side, continued to make sure that he knew whom he was talking to, and handed him bottles of water. Once more, he was given pain medication, and it did feel better, but he couldn't wait to get home to take something stronger.

Chapter 5

Jade watched Jenson as he struggled with waking up. She'd been giving him pain medication by way of an IV she'd put in for the last two days. He'd been in pain, anyone could see that, but once she was able to examine the wound on his leg, she made sure that he was in a deeper sleep so that she could put not only most of the stitches back in his leg but to carefully monitor the bruising that was covering nearly all of his thigh, front to back.

"Jade?" She told him that he was going to be all right. "I don't know what happened after we left the dinner. I'm assuming that I passed out."

"I helped with that. Not that I didn't want to hit

you, but I shot you up with Morphine so that you'd not hurt anymore. Why didn't you say something about how much pain you were really in." He said that it had been painful, but he'd been having a good time too. "The next time we go out, I might not help you along with meds to keep you upright."

"Will there be a next time we go out?" She nodded, not sure what to say to him about dating right now. "What happened? I mean, I'm druggy, feeling like I was before I left the hospital. I'm assuming you had to put in a few more stitches."

"Nearly all of them. Also, the bruising around the wound it a lot bigger than I was comfortable with, and I had you x-rayed as well as make sure that there was no infection in your body. Turns out you're just stubborn. I don't like you feeling bad, Jenson. I'd appreciate it if you didn't do this again. Piss me off so that I have to knock you around a bit." Jade couldn't help it. She'd been fighting tears for hours. But when he spoke to her, looking better than he had, she didn't hold back anymore but cried. "You can't be hurt again, Jenson. I love you, and seeing you in that much pain hurt me to my core. I'm so sorry that I hurt you."

"Come here, love." She didn't hesitate but got onto the bed with him. Making sure that she didn't bump his wound, she wrapped her arm over his chest and cried more. "I'm so sorry that I pissed you off enough that you had to hit me to get my attention. But I'm so happy to know that you love me too. I think I've loved you since the moment you stood up to me bullying you. You're my heart."

"Don't say things that your ass can't cover, Jenson. I've had a hard few days keeping you still, and I won't enjoy hearing you take it all back." He kissed her on the forehead. "That's nice. Thank you."

When she yawned twice, he simply held her. As her body began to relax in degrees, he held her to him. Jenson couldn't believe his luck in finding this woman just when he needed her the most. As he continued to hold her, he thought about a life with her. A life where the two of them could take care of each other forever.

He must have fallen asleep at some point because when he woke, he was alone in the big bed, and his dad was sitting in the chair next to the bed. Asking his dad where Jade went, his dad said that he'd never been so grateful for a pushy woman in his life.

"She kept us in line while you were out. She didn't bully us, but, well, you know how she can be. We were both sick with worry, and she made us get out of this room and to our own home until we looked like we'd had some sleep. I have to admit, I did feel much better after taking a long nap in my bed. These chairs aren't meant for sitting in for a long time." Jenson told his dad that he didn't even know where they came from. "I was thinking that you had a decorator come to your home. She was, I believe, trying to impress you with her...well, her wears rather than her talent. There are a lot of your rooms here that look good but aren't particularly comfy. Perhaps Jade will change things up for you."

"She loves me." Dad just stared at him. "I love her too. I don't know that it will go anywhere that would have her picking out furniture with me, but I've not been this happy and relaxed in some time."

"It shows on your entire body. You do seem to also be able to laugh more than you did before. Even if it's laughing at yourself. Something that I've not realized until I heard you doing it the other day that you've not done in some time. I missed that about you, son." He told him he was sorry. "No need for that. However, I'd like you to think about a couple of things while we're here alone. This woman, Jade, has a good head on her shoulders. I've looked into her little company, what she calls it, and she's doing extremely well. She invests well, works hard, and is good at seeing things outside the box. She and Clay have been working on some specialized tools for his job. I've not seen him so invested in his job as he is now."

"I like that about her too. She's also someone that I think I could depend on to make sure that I'm not lazy, either. She'll work no matter how much money we'd have. What's the second thing?" Dad told him. "Think about marrying her? I don't know, Dad. I mean, we've only known each other for a few weeks. Most of that has been with me laid up."

"You love her, don't you?" He said that he did with all his heart. "I'll tell you something, son. I love her too. So do your mom and your brothers. Not just because she's smart, but she's not like most of the women that you boys date. She's real. Original, I guess you could say. And she makes you happy."

"Those are all good reasons, dad, but what if

it's just a fling? What if, a few months or years down the road, we realize that we did things too quickly and that we're not suited? That would be bad for us both." Dad nodded and said that he was right. But brought up a point that he had been thinking about. "She would make a good congressman's wife. Jade would support me in all things, and I think she'd be helpful with things that come up too. Yes, I can see her being a part of that life. But still. It's only been a few weeks."

"You're right." Dad stood up, and he was afraid that he'd upset him. He told him he was sorry. "No need for that, son. Not at all. But I would like for you to do something for me. I want you to think of all the women you've seen and dated. Would any one of them be helpful for you to get to the White House as this young lady would?"

When dad left him, Jenson thought that his dad was making fun of him. He wasn't entirely sure how that was working, but he did what he asked. Starting with the last several women that he'd dated. All he could think about was how they'd wanted him to just spend money on them. Buy them nice things. One of them even wanted him to set her up in a house that she'd seen. It was bigger than the one that he had now. Not to mention, she wanted him to furnish it as well.

Her name had been Janice, if he remembered correctly. She'd done this thing with her eyes and lips that irritated the shit out of him. Even to this day, he wasn't sure why she thought that pushing out her lips like a fish and making her eyes wide and ugly had any effect on him, but she'd done it, and he hated it. Having her around too much, he realized, would have driven him bonkers.

There had been others too. All of them had thought that since he was rich, they were as well. One of them had even asked for his social security number so that she could get a credit card that would be attached to his accounts. Like he'd give her access to his bank because they were dating.

There were other women's troubles that he'd had too. Jenson, like all his brothers, was very careful about causal sex. They never had unprotected sex. Even if they had to walk away with a hard-on, they wouldn't allow anyone to catch them this way. Not that there were that many women that he slept with. Usually, after one or two dates, they began to show their true colors, and he would walk away. Not that that didn't have issues too.

He began to compare all women with Jade then. Not just their looks, because Jade was hands down the most beautiful of all of them but their ways about them. Jade didn't pout, didn't ask him for anything, nor did she treat him like he was a bank that had an endless supply of ready cash. While he did have a great deal of money, billions, he was careful how he spent it.

Jade didn't want anything from him. She'd never asked him for anything other than for him to be healthy. He was going to work on that too. Jade was smart as well. Not just with her job, but she'd been talking to his other brothers about what they were doing with their life.

Just this morning, Barton had come by to talk to him about a job that he wanted to take on. It was working with the school on an early morning program as well as an after-school one as well. He told him that Jade had said that a great many kids didn't get a hot meal until they had lunch at school. There might not even be a meal for them when they were home, either.

"I'm going to try and get some donations for getting it set up. I told her that I could use my own money to do that, but she said that if I did that, then people would have their hands out for every little thing that they needed. She's a smart cookie, that girl. If you don't marry her, I think I will." Barton laughed like he'd been in on a great joke, but the more that Jenson thought about having Jade as his wife, the more he loved the idea. Barton left him soon after, and he had time to wonder what the hell he was waiting on.

He knew that she was working today. Mom had told him when she'd been in earlier. Something about a project that would help elderly people get in and out of bed easier. He thought that if anyone could come up with the idea, it would be her. Using his cell phone, he called her. Jenson wasn't the least bit surprised when she answered the phone like they'd been talking all along.

"People should be made to live in a nursing home for a month before they allow their family to be in one. This woman I'm working with hasn't had a shower in four weeks. You can imagine how she smells." He told her he could imagine. "Christ, we'll have to give her the fucking bath anyway, even if we have to sedate her to do it." He asked her where she was. "A nursing home in Columbus. I know there aren't many places like this one, but I came in here without an appointment and caught the staff picking and choosing things off the resident's plates for themselves."

"Do you need for me to call someone on the resident's behalf? I have some really good connections that could help." She said that would be wonderful, and Jenson felt like a king. "I'll make the call right after I ask you something. Will you marry me?"

He knew that she was still on the line as he could hear things in the background. Waiting for a few more seconds, he asked her if she was all right. When she asked him to hold on, he could hear the noises fading in the background, and then a door shut.

"Isn't it customary for you to get down on one knee while I'm in the room with you? What would you have done if I had said yes? Would you have sent me a picture of how happy I've made you by agreeing to this lame assed proposal?" He laughed and asked her if she'd come here after she got back and he'd do it properly. "You get out of that bed before I tell you that you can, and I'll make myself a widow before I even get married to you."

"Is that a yes?" She said it was. "Christ, woman, you're never going to be anything but a pain in my ass, are you?"

"I'll work hard at that. Now, tell me if you were serious or not. Because if not, then you'd better be heading for the hills. I'm going to hunt you down and murder you if you were only kidding me." Jenson told her that he'd never been more serious about anything than having her as his wife. "Good. I'd love to be married to you. However, what will your family say about this? I mean, it's only been a short time since I hurt you and became a part of your sucky life."

"Dad told me that I should ask you. Also, my entire family likes you better than they do me." She told him that that's the way it should be. "I love you, Jade. So very much I don't want to spend another day without you in my life."

"I'd like that too. I'm thinking that we can't just shack up until we're married. Not with you having all this political shit going down." He said that if she wanted to move into his parent's home, they'd welcome her. "That might work better. I hate the house I got. I'm going to upgrade it in some places and rent it out. Also, it just occurred to me that you're going to need to have a big wedding."

"Why would…oh, the political shit I have going on. I never thought of that. Would that bother you?" She said not so long as they were married at the end of the day. "I couldn't agree more. If you come by here after you get finished working, I'll beg you to marry me again. With a beautiful ring too. However, if you don't like it, we can go for something else. It was my grandmother's. She left it to me in her will."

"As I said, so long as we're married, I don't care what happens beforehand." He heard a door open and figured that someone had been looking for her. "I have to go. I have shit going on here that I have to deal with. I don't know how late I'll be, but you make a few calls for me, and we'll work from there."

After closing the connection, he made two calls. He'd not been kidding when he said that he had some connections. Making the second call to the attorney general was like calling up an old friend. He was just as happy to hear that he was getting married as his parents were when he called them first thing.

~*~

Lisa was nervous about having Jade live with them until the wedding. Not for the girl herself, but she just didn't want to disappoint the young woman. Especially since she was going to be a part of their family. No date had been set or anything, but she had a feeling that it wouldn't be years in the making. She thought that they'd be lucky if their engagement lasted only a few weeks before they were demanding something quick. She'd been so excited to get a start on it that she was going to ask if Jade wanted her mother involved—hoping that she'd want to be—and they could get things going for the two of them.

"Lisa? Are you here?" She told Jade that she was in the kitchen. "I hope you don't mind, but when I told my mom that Jenson asked me to marry him, she wanted to come and meet you."

They came into the kitchen, the two of them, and Lisa instantly loved the other woman. After introductions were made, Hilda told her about her husband dying and that she was going to have a child. She then asked if she thought that would be an issue for the family.

"Good heavens, no. Have you planned on where you're going to be living with the child?" Hilda told her that Jade was going to raise him. If Jenson was up for that. "I'm sure he would love to raise him for you. You don't think you could do it?"

"I more than likely could, but I'm not able to. Not that I think of myself as being too old to have a child and raise it. But I am too old." They both laughed. "No. I want him to be able to be well taken care of and loved. Again, not that I won't love him, but I do want him to go to a loving home where I can see him. Jade was the first person that I thought of when I found out. I don't think that I'm mentally stable enough to raise a baby. I've had some depression issues."

"I can understand that completely. You've been dealt a tragic blow by your husband dying. I don't know what I'd do without Bar, my husband. He's my rock, along with my sons. And now Jade. I was hoping that we could get together and help her plan her wedding. I'm assuming that it will need to be large and lavish and quick."

"I don't know how lavish I can afford. Since she's my daughter, I'd like to be able to say that I'll pay for everything, but I don't have the funds for that." Jade assured her mom that she was going to pay for it, but she was going to help plan it all. "I can't do that, honey. What will people think of me?"

"You know me well enough that I don't give two shits what people will think of me. However, if anyone says one bad thing about you, they'll be on my shit list. It's not a long list, but I'll make sure that they never do that again." Lisa was glad to see that Jade and her mother got along. They might not have a mother/daughter relationship like most, but they were good together. As they were talking about some of the things that Jade wanted on a wedding day, Lisa began making notes.

"Did you have a dress in mind? I so wish that I had one that you could wear, but when I married my husband, we both wore jeans and tee shirts." Hilda looked at her. "I bet you have a lovely dress that you wore."

"I do. And I'd be honored if you wished to use it." She wanted to sob when she thought of Jade wearing her gown. She'd only had sons, so knowing that one of the brides of them would wear it made her so very happy. "I will pull it out here in just a moment. Of course, you'll stay for dinner tonight,

Hilda." She said that she'd like that. But didn't want to intrude. "There isn't any way that you'll ever be considered an intruder. We'll have a nice dinner, and then we'll see what the wedding dress will need for Jade to decide on it."

Jade had asked if she thought that Barton would do the invitations. "I know he does calligraphy for menus and such. Do you think you could ask him for us?" Lisa said that he'd do it, but it might mean more if she were to ask him. "How about I just tell him to do it? That'll be more in line with how I treat people."

They enjoyed their time together, and when the other two followed her up to the bedroom where her dress was, she was sentimental in pulling the gown out for Jade and her mom to see. Lisa was glad that she'd had it cleaned and boxed up all those years ago.

"Now, you can change it in any way that you wish. I'm not sure how up-to-date it is with other wedding dresses, but I'm sure that it'll have to be taken in here and there." Jade stared at the dress that she'd hung on the back of the closet door. "My bridesmaids were dressed all in shades of blues. The men, their ties matched the dresses. Bar wore a white tux too. He was all in white like I was." She pulled out her photo album as Jade continued to stare at the dress. It was making her slightly nervous. "This was before cell phones were around so much, and this is all the pictures that were taken that day. During the reception, someone did have a video recorder. I think those tapes are stuffed away in that closet too."

"Lisa, would you mind very much if I tried the dress on?" She shook her head and watched as Jade stripped down to her panties without any thought as to who was in the room with her. After buttoning up the back for her, Jade asked where a mirror was. "I need to see this on me. I have a feeling that it's going to be the most perfect wedding dress that anyone could ever wear."

She did look so very lovely in the gown. There were no sleeves on the dress. There had been when she'd picked it out, but Lisa hated the over-the-top lace of it. The front had a little lace on it that went up and around her neck. If she'd had to do it over, Lisa would have taken even that bit of lace off. It was itchy and hot. But the rest of the gown was a perfect fit for her future daughter-in-law. When Jade said that she didn't care for the lacy front, telling her the same thing that she'd felt when she'd worn it, Lisa laughed.

"I was going to suggest that. Small straps can be added to hold it up for you, but the lace will itch you to death once it gets hot. It fits you in length too. What sort of shoes would you wear? I'm thinking that you could forgo heels and just wear pretty flats. You and Jenson are so tall it will be doubtful if anyone would notice your lack of shoes if you were to go barefooted." She said she'd like flats so as not to distract from the dress. "Honey, no one will remember that dress once you have your hair done and make-up."

"I agree with Lisa on that. You're so lovely, Jade. You make this poor mom of yours so happy." After helping her daughter with the veil that had come with the dress, Hilda cried so gently she was sure to join her. "Oh, Jade. I never dreamed that you'd be such a lovely happy bride. And that I'd be here to witness it."

After calling someone to do the alterations later, it was settled that the dress would be perfect. The only thing that had to be done to it was, of course, the neckline fixed. Also, two of the Swarovski buttons needed to be replaced as Bar had pulled them free, and they couldn't find them.

By the time the boys showed up with Jenson, he was in a wheelchair, dinner was on its way to being finished. She was glad now that she'd had Bar pick up the ring from the cleaners for her so that they could all be there when he asked her. Officially anyway.

No one asked what they'd been doing all afternoon. She was thrilled to know that Jenson would be surprised about his wife wearing his mother's dress. Lisa was also happy that the two of them would be having such a luxurious wedding.

After handing Jenson the ring, he moved himself over to where Jade was sitting on the couch. Not that he was planning on getting out of the chair, but they all watched as he asked Jade to marry him. Lisa had a hard time controlling herself when Jade said that she'd marry him. The ring, like the dress, fit her like it had been made just for her.

"You've made me the happiest man on earth right now," Jade told him ditto. It was the perfect thing to say so that they were laughing instead of on the verge of tears. When each of the boys hugged

Jenson and kissed Jade, they sat around the living room and talked about dates. She'd been correct in thinking that it wouldn't be that long from now. They picked a date one month from today. New Year's Eve. So that they could start the new year out as husband and wife.

"I want you to go through the house with me. I was thinking that it needs to be less like a showcase and more like a home. I never noticed it before dad said how uncomfortable the chairs were in the room I'd been in. Also, I'm not sure even how old the mattress is in the master suite. I think it's at least twenty years old as I had it when I was a kid and loved it so much I brought it over for me to use."

As they talked about the house, Lisa sat by her husband. It was happening, she thought. Her boys would not need her as much. Leaning her head on his shoulder, he asked her what she was thinking about. After telling her, he did something that he'd not done in years, he tweaked her nose.

"What you should be thinking about is grandchildren from them. I can see them having a child within the year. Then they'll pop them out every couple of years. The two of them are in so much love now that I wonder if they realize that there are others in the room." She told him about the dress and what Jade had said about it. "Did you tell her why two buttons are missing? I'm sure that she was able to guess."

"She just smiled at me in that knowing way." Bar laughed, and that drew the attention of the others to them. Instead of explaining when asked, she told them that dinner was ready, and they all went to the dining room. There was no way that she was going to tell her grown children that their father had been so impatient to have her that he'd ripped all forty-one buttons off with his bare hands.

Dinner was much like it had been when the boys were all living at home. Loud with threats to each other and laughter. Jade and her mother brought it all together with them, and she thought they enjoyed it as much as she did.

Lisa thought it was wonderful to see her son in love. He could barely take his eyes off Jade but didn't crowd her. Not that Lisa thought that she'd allow him to do that. They were perfectly suited to each other. When her husband asked for champagne and apple juice for Hilda, he made a toast that was something along the lines that her father had done for her and Bar.

"I'm a proud father right now. Not that I haven't been since the day all my sons were born. But to bring a lovely and wonderfully amazing daughter-in-law to the family makes me feel like I could conquer the world." He looked at Jenson before continuing. "Son, my heart is full right now. It can only be fuller that the two of you are blessed with many children. And happiness for the rest of your lives." Jade stood up.

"As most all of you know now, my mom is going to have a child. After talking with Jenson, we're going to adopt my half-brother and raise him as our own. With my mother's blessings." Lisa looked around at her other sons as Jade continued. "I can only hope that someday soon, you meet your other halves and be as happy as we are right now. So get up off your asses and get out there and meet someone."

Lisa was still laughing about the look on her son's face when she went up to bed later that night. Jade and her mom were staying tonight so that they could get an early start on tomorrow's list, and Lisa had never been as happy as she was at this very moment.

Chapter 6

Herbert wasn't having any fun. He thought that since he was from a wealthy family, he should be able to have special treatment. Of course, that hadn't gotten him anywhere but in trouble. Even his meals, which were shit to begin with, were worse than they'd been before. Who the hell thought a sandwich was good enough for someone like him? No one, that's who.

The officer that had brought him to the courthouse thought it was funny that he wanted to have a suit to put on instead of the pus green jumper that he had been wearing. Even when he told them to bill it to his mother if they weren't going to pay for it got him nothing but laughter directed at him. Christ, the world was coming to an end, and he wasn't going to be sitting on the sidelines to watch but right in the middle of the shit storm.

"Mr. Pauly, are you paying attention?" He said that he was thinking about his mother and why she wasn't getting him out of this predicament that he was in. "Aren't you a little old to be thinking that your mother is going to be bailing you out? However, it's my understanding that she helped get you caught. Mr. Strong, you might want to enlighten Mr. Pauly here on his mother's activities of late."

"Yes, sir." Mr. Strong, the bastard that was thinking that he was going to be changing his mother's will, moved to the front of the room in a wheelchair. The shithead was getting weaker all the time if he'd gone from crutches to a wheelchair. "Mrs. Pauly has sold her home and has been on a cruise ship enjoying herself since the day that you were arrested. As you were told, Mr. Pauly, you've been removed from her will, and she has disowned you in all ways. Also, she had made it clear that you are responsible for your expenses and that she has cut off all credit that you had while living in her home."

"You're a liar." Mr. Strong said that he was not. "You have to be. There is no way that—I'm her only child, damn it. What the hell is she going to do with all that money that my father left her."

"Your father didn't have any money when he married Mrs. Pauly. She made all her riches before she married him. There was also a prenup that he signed as well." He told him that his father had died. "I'm well aware of that, Mr. Pauly. I was just telling you that your father didn't leave anything to your mother. She already owned it. Your mother is a very wealthy woman."

"I'm going to be as well when she dies. Christ, this is stupid. I want you to change everything back to the way it was. I'll make it worth your while when she's gone." No one said anything, and Herbert looked at the judge. "What now? You look like you've been given an all-day sucker."

"You just tried to bribe someone. Right here in my courtroom." Herbert asked him what the big deal was. "The big deal is that it's against the law."

"So what? Everyone does it. Why not have it right out there in the open." He turned back to Mr. Strong. "What do you say? Mom won't have to know.

She'll be dead by then. And I'll make sure that you are well compensated for your troubles."

"No thanks." He looked at the judge then. "I'd like to press additional charges against Mr. Pauly for trying to get me to change his mother's will. Other charges go along with that charge that I'll write up for you as soon as I get back to my office."

Not only was he taken back to the van he'd arrived in, but he was taken back to the cell he'd been in. Asking the officer what was going on, he was told nothing. When asked if he could call his mother, again, he was ignored. This was just getting stupid. Why were they treating him like he was the bad guy in all this?

When his dinner came, he just let it sit in the little opening of his cell. He could smell the fish from where he was sitting. While he did like the dinners that they brought him, he was going to protest by not eating until he got things going his way.

How could his mother disown him? That was the ten-cent question. He was her only child. There had to be laws about being able to do something like that. And why did she sell off his house? Didn't she think that he was going to need a place to live when she got him out of here? Women just didn't think beyond what was in front of them. His dad used to say that all the time.

He thought about his father not having any money when he married Herbert's mom. Women didn't have a head for money. That Strong person had it all wrong. But the more he thought about it, the more times he could remember his father being yelled at by his mother. For spending money willy-nilly. Whatever the hell that meant. If she had money, then he had money. Like it was between the two of them. His mother had a great deal of money which in turn meant that he did as well. What was wrong with his mom that she wasn't on board with the way things should always be? Women.

Herbert remembered his father drinking a great deal. He wasn't a mean drunk like most of his friends' fathers, but he wasn't all that friendly either. Dad had hit his mom once and only that one time. She'd pulled out a gun from her pocket and shot him right in the leg with it. Christ, his dad had bellowed like a wounded cat about that. But he never hit her again.

Dad would talk to him about his plans. Good

solid plans too. Like buying up the air over fields. Nobody was using it, and dad had told him that it could be used for sending airwaves across the world. He'd never been able to figure out how to sell it, however. Dad told him when he'd been turned down for a loan at the bank that no one saw things the way he did. Herbert had. And still did, as a matter of fact.

His latest idea had been to take all the clothing that was going for the shelter and make people cut them up into strips and weave out some rugs. He had a woven rug in his bedroom that he loved more than the carpet that was in the rest of the house. Every time he looked at it, he'd see a new color or a mistake in it that he'd have to point out every time someone came into his room. No one appreciated him and his knowledge about such shit.

When he'd brought it up to his mom, his rug idea, she asked him what the homeless or needy were to wear if he had them cut the donated clothing up. He asked her why that should be his problem when he had an idea that was going to work.

"No, it won't work. People will stop donating the clothing if you're going to be selling these rugs. I'm assuming that you'd not pay the homeless and needy for making them." He said why should he. They were living at the shelter for free. "So you want to make a profit off of someone else's hard work, do you? Without any cost to you or effort. That's not the way charities work, you know that, don't you? You shouldn't make a profit off of donated items."

"I've looked it up. There are a lot of companies that make a killing off of someone else doing all the work. Like your dress business. You make money off of it, don't you?" She said that she did, but she paid her employees. "You're a sap, mother. Why are you paying people when they should be lucky to have a job."

"How is it lucky to have a job when they're working for free? Herbert, do you even understand how commerce works? The word means the activity of buying and selling. There would be no workers if they weren't getting paid. That people need to be productive and paid for their work, or nothing gets done?" He said that she was messing up his plan by talking about paying people all the time. "I'm sorry that you feel that way. But I pay my people working for me so that they'll keep coming to work every day and be productive and good workers. So, in answer to your earlier question? No, I'm not going to give you money to start your rug business. You won't last long enough for you to pay me back."

"Pay you back? Why would I have to do that?" She said that when she helps with plans, she expects to get money in return. "That would eat into my profits. That's not right."

She never listened to his ideas again after that. She'd asked him upfront if he was planning on paying her back. When he said no, she'd just walk away. His dad listened, however. That was why he'd been so close to him. Not only did his dad listen to his ideas, but he would help him expand on them and make them even better. But they never got a single dime from mom to make them millionaires like they both should have been.

When the man came back to take his tray, he didn't say a word about him not eating it. As soon as it was gone, Herbert wanted to call him back so that he could eat it. He never put it together that if you don't eat, then you're going to be hungry. Since he'd never been hungry a day in his life, then he'd never experienced having an empty belly before.

By the time the lights were turned out, he was

sure he was going to die of starvation. Christ, he wished now that he'd at least eaten a part of the meal. Even drinking out of the facet at the sink in the cell wasn't helping fill out the void he was experiencing.

Herbert didn't think that he had slept a wink all night. Not only did he have hunger pangs throughout the night, but he was also riddled with pain in his chest as well as his head. Who knew that food did so much for a body?

By the time the sun came up, shining brightly through his window, he was sick with a headache as well as he was sure that he was going to bust his kidneys because he'd been drinking water so much. Now he had to piss, and he was afraid of standing up, sure he was going to fall over he was weak with the fact that no one would bring him anything to eat.

As soon as his tray was slid under his cell door, Herbert grabbed it up and started eating everything that was on it. Avoiding the bottled water, he did eat the three slices of toast, all at once with nothing on them other than butter. He usually ate only jam on his toast, but he was too hungry to slow down enough to do that.

The coffee, usually lukewarm, was scalding

hot when he drank it down. The eggs weren't to his taste, they had scrambled them up with bits of ham and onions again, but that didn't stop him from cramming them into his mouth as quickly as he had the other things on the tray. However, almost as soon as it all hit his belly, he was at the commode throwing up everything that he'd just shoved in his mouth.

Herbert laid back on the floor as he waited on his belly to rebel again. He wasn't just sick with this but hurting too. Knowing too that he'd be sore tomorrow from throwing up so much. Lying there, waiting to die, he supposed, someone was speaking to him from the front of his cell. Since his head was still aching, he just told them to go away.

"I'm here to take you out of here, Mr. Pauly. Get whatever you want to take with you gathered up." That perked him up a bit, and he gingerly moved to a sitting position. "You're being remanded over to Federal prison for tax evasion. Among other things too. Will you tell me your full name and birthdate?"

"Will you leave me alone if I don't provide you with that?" He said he'd just take him anyway, and if he was the wrong person, someone would shoot him. "Shot me? Whatever for. I don't even understand why this is all such a big deal. I've done nothing wrong when I know that there are thousands of people out there that have done the same thing."

"However, you were caught. And believe it or not, that is all it takes. Now, are you going to confirm your date of birth and full name, or do I drag you out of here by your hair?" He stood up and had to hang onto the wall for a moment to steady himself. Herbert told the man that he'd not eaten much. "I heard that you turned your nose up to just about anything they brought you, and last night you didn't eat. Making a pig of yourself didn't make you feel any better, now, did it?"

Once he was in the van, locked down again so that he'd not fall over, they told him. Which he thought was a lie. The three men with him weren't locked in, and they seemed to be staying upright. Of course, they were holding onto guns and ready to no doubt blast his head off if he tried something.

Thinking about his mother on a cruise without him pissed him off. How dare she leave him to fend for himself. Not only that, but to sell her house without taking into account his needs? It wasn't at all motherly of her, was all he could say about that.

She'd better be saving every dime of the sale so that he could get out of this mess he was in. While wanting to blame it all on her, he couldn't. It was the system that had gotten him this time. And their too many rules.

Herbert hated all manner of people right now. Not just the stupid man in front of him but every cock sucker he'd ever met in his entire life that had to give him a hard time. They acted like they were so much superior to him. Smarter too.

He liked to think of himself as the ideal man. Not the planner. He could see the end product of his ideas but nothing to do with the execution and especially not about making it work once it was started. His mom had always called him lazy. Herbert had always told her that it was exhausting thinking all the time. And it was.

What he needed was a good attorney to get him out of this mess and anything else that he got himself into. One that would do what he wanted when he needed it done. Herbert wondered if it was possible to sue his mother. Surely someone would think that was a wonderful idea. Or better yet, sue that Strong guy. He was weak and stupid. Herbert thought that he could get a lot of money from him just to settle out of court. Yeah, that's what he wanted someone to do for him. Sue the Strong family and have them settle out of court.

He'd work on that the moment he was given his phone call. Herbert wasn't above greasing a couple of palms to get what he wanted, but he didn't have the grease to make that happen yet. He would. As soon as his mother got off her high horse and got her skinny ass back here to help him out. Damn it all to fuck and back. Being stuck in jail was making it so that he was getting very little done.

By the time he was at the new jail, which to him had looked more like a prison, he had it all worked out in his head. Not a lot of details yet on how that was going to come to work, but he had the ending all lined up. People would be begging him to take their money when he was finished with his mother and her cock sucking attorney. Just see that they didn't. Yes, Herbert thought, things might well work out yet.

~*~

Jenson had been doing everything right since he'd been engaged to Jade. Staying off his leg, resting a great deal, and making sure that he had his crutches nearby when he only wanted to get in and out of the bathroom. He'd even hired staff to help out around the house when the daily crew was gone for the day. Things were beginning to look very homey around the home he was going to be sharing with Jade, and he couldn't be happier.

If only he could get her to come to his bedroom at some point, he'd show her all the things that he'd been missing to do to her. Then there were the things that he'd been making up in his head that he thought they'd both enjoy. When a short knock came at his office door, he looked up and saw Jade. She looked good enough to eat. And he wanted to in the worse sort of way.

"I have two questions for you. One of them has nothing to do with the other, but I need answers. Did you make arrangements at the bank for me to be on your accounts? If so, what does that mean exactly?" He said that his money was hers now. "I thought that you'd say that. So you have to go to the bank to sign papers that say the same about the money that I have. By the way, what do you know of the banker in town? He's sort of slimy, don't you think?"

"Is that the second question?" She laughed and told him it was only an observation. "Slimy? I'm not sure that I've spent that much time with him to be able to say for sure. However, if you think he is, then I believe you. I should run a background check on him now, anyway. I'm sure that the bank has in their time, but I need one now so that I don't have a slimy shit handling our money. What else did you want to know?"

"Can you fuck me?" He nearly swallowed his tongue. Whole. When he asked her to repeat herself, she did. "I'm sick of sleeping alone. Not that I've not done that my entire life, but I know that you're not far away, and I want to…well, I guess I'd not be sleeping with you but fucking your brains out. I find that I'm needy when I'm around you, but there are always about a dozen people around too. How about this? I lock this door, and we have a little bit of fun getting to know one another biblically?"

"Come here, Jade." She moved across the room but went back to the door. He was sure that she was teasing him and Jenson thought he'd cry if she was. But she locked the door, then pulled one of the chairs over to it and stuck the back of it under the handles.

Closing the curtains too, the room had a soft glow to it that he thought was romantic.

Jade got down on the floor in front of his wheelchair. When she sat up on her knees and began undoing his belt buckle, he was glad that it didn't require him to answer when she started talking. He wasn't sure that he could have anyway.

"I have had sex before. It wasn't all that enjoyable. I think that was mostly my fault. I wanted my head to explode when I came, but all I got was a little buzz. Nothing to write home about." She had his pants undone and his cock out when she leaned over and kissed the tip of him. "I knew that you'd be thick and long. Long enough for me to have a happy dance when I come, I'm betting."

"I sure hope I can make you very happy." She grinned at him and quickly leaned over, and took the crown of his cock into his mouth. "Mother fuck, Jade, that's amazing."

While she bobbed over his cock, he moved his hips so that he could free himself from his pants. He'd been wearing loose-fitting gym pants to make it easier to get in and out of. It had worked well so far, but this was a bonus that he'd not thought of.

She made short work of his pants by pulling them down off his legs to the floor. His injured leg was feeling so much better. In fact, he was in no pain at all right now, so he laid his foot gently on the floor so as not to ruin the moment they were having.

Her fingers were warm over his balls. Jade's mouth was hot and slick, and he enjoyed raising his hips so that he could go deeper into her throat. Passing the tight muscles in the back of her throat had him coming, but it wasn't as fulfilling as he'd hoped. However, Jade was just getting started, so he waited for her next move. And the next move was meant to kill him. He was positive of that.

Standing up, she stripped off her clothing and stood before him. As she let her fingers glide down her breast, tweaking her nipples until they were hard, he couldn't swallow. His mouth was so dry. As she made her way down her hips and over her navel, he licked his lips in anticipation of her touching her center. A place that he wanted to be. Her moan echoed through his head when she slid her fingers deep into the dark curls at her pussy.

"Oh yes, baby. Make yourself come for me." Wrapping his hand around his cock, Jenson watched as she slid her fingers in and out of herself. Juices ran down her thighs as he watched her. With her other hand, she rolled her nipples around, making them and himself harder with each beat of his heart. "Come for me, Jade."

She screamed out his name. As she rode her fingers, he felt his cock erupt with his climax. His cum shot up so high that it hit her on her face, breasts, and her lips. Wanting more, no, needing more, Jenson reached for her just as she was moving forward. Sitting her on his desk after shoving everything he'd been working on to the floor, he buried his face into her pussy and drank greedily from her.

Her feet ended up on the arms of his wheelchair, giving him access to all of her. Sliding his fingers into her, Jenson was rewarded with more of her juices, more moans, and screams from her. When he knew she was going to come, her body stiffening, he nipped at her clit and welcomed so much juice from her that he was sure it was running down his face.

"Fuck me, Jenson." Pulling her off the desk, she slid over his cock. Neither of them moved for a few seconds until she took his mouth hard in a hungry kiss. Fucking her by bringing her body to his with his hands, Jenson suckled at her breasts, taking pleasure from her needs until she screamed at him that she was coming.

Her face was beautiful in her coming. Her breasts were pinked by his beard and teeth. Even as she rode him hard, telling him to come with him, all Jenson could think about was that Jade was his. Forever and a day. However, all thought went out the window when she bit at his earlobe, bringing him to the here and now and to a climax himself. Christ, he was going to be sore for a year when he let go.

The climax stopped his heart. He couldn't hear either. Even his breaths were hard to get going again when he finally found a way to express how hard he was coming. Holding onto Jade, not sure if she was going to be with him when he died in a few moments, Jenson let his eyes roll to the back of his head, and he just simply blinked out.

Waking up with Jade's head on his shoulder and her breaths warming his skin, Jenson ran his hands up and down her back to give himself a few minutes before he might be required to speak. While not sure what he'd say even if he could speak, all he could think about was that he was in love. Not just with Jade but everything about her. And he would be forever too.

"I think I'm busted." He laughed at her when she finally spoke. She'd not moved yet. For which he was grateful. If she moved her hips even a tiny bit, he was going to sob. Like a five-year-old without a nap. "Why the hell did we wait so long to do this?"

"More than likely because we knew that we'd be incapacitated for hours afterward. I don't know about you, but I think that if we do this even twice a week, we're going to be old before our time. I mean, like ancient old. I'm going to hurt when you move too." She looked at him, and Jenson smiled. "I love you so much, Jade."

"And I love you. However, I have a kink in my leg, and if I don't move soon, I'm going to be hurting worse." She moved quickly. Much quicker than he thought that he could have under the circumstances. She did hobble to the couch that was in his office before grabbing up his shirt that he'd only just realized had been removed and pulled over her body. Disappointment and relief moved over him. "I'm aware that you have to keep up appearances because of the political path that you're taking, but

I'm going to empty the house at least once a day so that I can jump you like this. Do you think it will be better in a bed?"

"Christ, I hope not. I don't think I'll survive you if it is." They both laughed. "I'm going to get my pants back on and see about getting us something to snack on before dinner." She said that they were the only ones in the house. "You did kick everyone out?"

"No, not really. The cook needed to go to the store to set up the home delivery. Her husband, Samuel, said he had some errands to run and asked me if I'd keep an eye on you. I told him that we had things to discuss concerning the wedding, and he winked at me as he left. I figured that if he came back to all the screams in here, he would know not to disturb us. I like him, by the way."

"I do as well. He was my dad's butler until I was born, then he became my man in waiting. I don't know that they call it that anymore but he helped me learn how to be a man when I was out with my parents and back then, my grandparents."

"My mom wasn't around all that much when I was a child. My informative years, I guess you could call them. But there was this lady that lived across the street from us that would invite me over for a visit. She was the one that showed me how to be a refined woman, she called me. Also, how to make and drink a good hot cup of tea as well as eat with the right fork when I sat down for dinner. For a long time, I had it in my head she was grooming me for someone she knew, but she was just a nice lady that took pity on a lonely child." Jenson said that was nice of her. "When she died, she left me the tea set as well as her collection of tea cups and teas. I still have them. Boxed up in a storage place with a lot of other things that I've collected over the years. I travel a great deal, and I would find myself a place to pick up something unique while I was there. A teacup. A book. Something that would remind me of the place. I wonder if you'd mind if I brought them here to put out."

"This is your house, babe. You bring in anything that you want." She kissed him on the mouth as he rolled by her. "When do you think that I can get out of this chair and move around with crutches? I'm sick of being tied to this thing."

"If you promise to behave yourself and not overdo it, you can use the cane. However, I want you to sit when you're tired. Rest when you need to and not put it off. I don't want to have to—I was going to say tie you to the bed, but that sounds good to me." After getting his cane, the two of them went into the kitchen. He had to be careful walking, it had been a few days since he'd tried, but he was happy that he wasn't on his ass all the time and able to see above the table now. Laughing with her at the little bit of food in the fridge, they had some carrots and dip that had been left over from dinner last night. Christ, Jenson was happy as he'd been in some time with Jade at his side.

"Lisa called me at work today. She wanted to know if we'd like to have dinner with her and Bar tonight. I'm glad I remembered. I told her that it would be up to you." He said that he'd love that. "Good. Also, our invitations went out today. I think your brother did a fantastic job on them. Don't you?"

"I do. I can't believe it's only going to be three and a half weeks before we're married. I've been looking for honeymoon destinations on the computer while I'm waiting on someone to return my call. I'm thinking that we go to Europe and see the place together."

They talked about their wedding and honeymoon after he called his mom. Dad said that he'd been hungry for a steak for a couple of days and a baked potato with all the trimmings. Jenson thought his dad had a brilliant idea, and they set up the plans to go with them.

Chapter 7

Clay used the tool three times before he decided that it was a perfect fit for his hand. Jade had come over with it yesterday after him telling her what he needed it to do the day before. Not only had she added the things that he'd asked for, like the storage for the extra battery, but she'd also incorporated a longer charging cord as he'd asked her about.

"Hey, Clay. I was wondering if you'd be all right with me leaving a little early tonight. My sister and her family are coming over for dinner, and my wife just sent me a list of things that I need to pick up. She has like ten kids, and they're all grubby little monsters." Clay told him that it would be fine with him if he left early. He didn't much care for the other man anyway, and the more he was able to not work with him, the better his day would be. "Thanks. I owe you. Maybe I'll bring you a plate of food tomorrow. For all her brats, she can sure cook up a storm when she wants."

"My mom stocked me up yesterday. I have plenty of leftovers." He didn't, but he wasn't going to take anything from this man or his family. "You have fun with your family, and I'll see you on Monday."

It had only occurred to him an hour ago that it was Friday and not Thursday, as he'd been thinking it was all day. After getting the tools that Martin got out and didn't put away, he cleaned up his area. Tomorrow was going to be a good day, he thought. Clay had an interview with some higher-ups at NASA.

Twice a week for the last month, he'd been getting calls from NASA. Jade told him that since they were working together, he'd have to be cleared for Top-Secret clearance. He'd thought that he had that already, but she informed him that he was only at Secret clearance and not the top like she was. Every day Clay learned something new about his soon-to-be sister-in-law that impressed him each time.

The other day she'd called him to a site where she was working so that he could help her. It wasn't like she needed him, he found out later, but she wanted him to meet a few of her clients. Someone that had ties with the White House. Ties so deep, he'd found out that he'd been speaking to the Vice President himself for an hour before it occurred to him who it was.

The door behind him opened and closed, and he thought it was Martin returning for something he'd forgotten. The man usually had to come back three times before he left the office, forgetting one thing or another before he was set to go home.

When he smelled the distinct smell of a woman's perfume, he turned around. He couldn't believe the beauty that was standing before him. She smiled at him and asked him something. Clay didn't have a clue what she'd asked him, but he nodded anyway.

"Is there something wrong with you?" Clay told her that he was stunned to silence by her beauty. "Yeah, right. I'm looking for my brother, Martin. He said that he works here."

"He left early for a visit from his sister. You?"

She said that Martin had five sisters, and she was only one of them. "Do you have brats? I'm sorry, I mean children?"

"That would be Melody. Her kids are brats. But then, so is Melody. I'm Rachel. I have no attachments, children, or much to do with my family. You must be Clay Strong." He put out his hand and had an overwhelming urge to pull her to him for a long, much-needed kiss when she shook his hand. "You're one of the Strong men that are as rich as Midas. I have no idea what that means, but I've heard it all my life."

"Yes, I'm one of six, not including my parents. I'm sure you've heard this before, but you're beautiful. Nothing at all like your brother." She thanked him with a laugh. "I'm sorry, that didn't come out right. You are very beautiful, and for some reason that I can't explain, I want to kiss you." She took a step back from him. "I'm sorry. I didn't mean to frighten you."

"I have to go. If you see my brother, tell him that I'm leaving tonight for Washington. I won't be coming back here." He asked her if she was all right. "No. Stay away from me, Mr. Strong. I won't be happy if you—"

"Now wait a damned minute here. I didn't do anything to you to deserve you being a bitch all of a sudden. I only said that I wanted to kiss you. I didn't act on that." She moved back further from him. "What is your issue? You came here to my office, and I did nothing wrong for you to be treating me like I'm a rapist or something."

When she left him there without another word, he wanted to chase her down and find out what the hell her problem was. He'd done nothing wrong other than to tell her that he wanted to kiss her. He'd not done it. Her reaction was well beyond what was called for, and he decided that he was going to talk to her brother about her behavior on Monday.

He wasn't in a kind mood to work anymore, so he packed up his things and made his way home. Just as he was just sitting down to his leftovers when someone pounded on his door. Going to see who the hell they were, he opened the door and flew back when someone punched him in the face. Hard enough to knock him out on his ass too.

Waking up, his defenses still in flight or fight mode, he realized that he was in the hospital. His mom was in the room with him, and he asked her what was going on. She cried, telling him that she was so glad that he was all right.

"I remember opening my door, then nothing else." She said that Martin Jameson had been arrested for assault and battery. That he'd been there to defend his sister. "Yeah, I remember her. She's off her rocker."

"Be that as it may, she isn't none too happy with you either. Something about you making a pass at her. I guess she told her brother, and he went to your house to give you a lesson in treating his women, I kid you not, Clay, that's what he said. Who is that man?" he told her that they worked together. "Well, I hope he gets fired. The man deserves no less than that than knocking you out. You have a concussion too."

He was hurting badly enough to call for something mild for pain. When the nurse entered, handing him the pills, she spoke to his mom. Once she left the room, he asked what was going on.

"How much do you know about Martin?" Clay told his mom that they'd only been working together for the last six months. "Nothing personal?"

"What's going on?" She started to pace, something that he'd never seen her do before. When she paused and turned to look at him, he wasn't sure that he wanted to know what she was going to say to him. "It's bad, isn't it?"

"Not really. Martin and Rachel are the same people." He started to tell her that she was wrong about that, but she continued before he could say anything. "Martin has been diagnosed with multiple personalities since he was a child. There are several others that he has in his head. One of them would be a sister that has four children. I'm not at all sure how that works with there being no children around, but Jade told me that he shouldn't have been working with you on the projects that you have going on. He's a danger in that he has no control over who comes around."

"How did Jade find out? I'm sure that she's right, but what tipped her off." Mom told him what she'd figured out when she was at his job site the other day. "What did?"

"She said that he would flip in and out of being Martin to one of his other personalities. Twice, she said that he told her that she was too pretty, prettier than she was. It took her all of five minutes to figure out what he was dealing with." He asked her what was going to happen now. "He's going to lose his job, of course. Not because of his illness but because he hit you. Also, and this should have been addressed long ago if you were to ask me, he hasn't been taking his medications regularly. Like it has been months since he's picked up any of the meds that he's on from the pharmacy."

"This isn't anything that I expected you to say. But I will admit, I did find him to be a beautiful woman when he was talking to me. And his or her personality was so much different than Martin's that I thought that I'd like to hang out with her. Or him. I'm not sure how that works." He leaned back on the bed and smiled at his mother. "You're my hero, Mom. I don't think that we, any of us, tell you how much we love you enough."

"Thank you, son. I needed to hear that today." She sat down. "Jade and her mom are going to go to a cake tasting event this afternoon. If you think you can behave yourself, then I'm going to leave you here. They're going to discharge you soon, so long as you're with someone. So your dad is coming in to take you home and watch over you. Please try not to get your noodle knocked around anymore, Clay. It's too much on my heart. What with you being hurt and Jenson too, it's too much for my tender heart."

"You have the heart of a lion, and I dare anyone to say anything differently. I love you so much, Mom." She kissed him on the cheek and left him there after telling him how much she loved him too. After she left him, he called his dad to tell him that he was ready to go when they released him. "Mom and the other women are going to go cake testing. Why isn't Jenson going too? Won't he get to eat the cake?"

"He's going to meet them there later. Right now, he's at a luncheon for some women's group. I was invited, too, but I don't think I'd be much use to him with a bunch of women shooting questions at him about his upcoming wedding. You know how women love a good love story." Clay laughed, then held his head. "I'll be there soon, son. Also, after I get you, we'll get some unhealthy lunch for us."

The doctor came in as he was putting his phone away. After telling him what he needed to do to be safe, his discharge paperwork was given to him, and he signed off to go home. Getting dressed was a little difficult as every time he bent over, his head hurt, but he was ready to go when his dad arrived.

They did have a very unhealthy lunch. It started with a slice of pie, each with ice cream and whipped cream, then they ordered loaded fries, each with a sub. He didn't realize how hungry he was until they sat his food down in front of him. Dad laughed when he told him that he was going to have to start running again. Dad had been running in the morning since he'd been old enough to notice. They made plans to do it together when he was fit.

Barkley joined them soon after they started eating. Clay had forgotten what a flirt he could be when he wanted something. Not only did he get his meal in record time, but he set up a date with the waitress for that night. Clay realized that he'd not been on a date in months and decided to take care of that as soon as he was feeling better. He missed having a female around to talk to.

Going to his parent house to hang out with his dad, he sat on the couch and promptly fell asleep. He didn't know if it was the stress or just all the carbs that he'd had for lunch, but Clay was exhausted. He didn't even care that he should be making plans for his interview in the morning. He just needed some sleep.

~*~

Jenson was glad that he was able to duck out of the lady's luncheon at a reasonable time. He wanted to spend as much time with his future wife as he could. Of course, she fussed at him about how he was overdressed, but he didn't care. Kissing her on the mouth, an easy way to make her smile, he picked up his fork and tried the first slice of cake that Jade said she'd narrowed it down to.

"It's fruit cake. I'm not sure that I've ever had fruit cake that tasted like this. But the chef said that more and more people are mixing their layers up so that everyone can get a bit of something that they like. Whatever. It's our wedding, and if they don't like our cake, then they can go home." He laughed, as he did all the time when he was with her. "Your mom likes the orange slice cake. But my mom said she thinks it's too sweet. What do you think?"

"I don't like orange slices." She asked him to try it, and he was completely surprised that he liked it. "Okay, I don't like orange slices that aren't wrapped around cake batter. I love this. But it is a bit sweet."

He didn't care for the chocolate and cherries. Neither had the mothers. Jade said that she was taste-tested out, and he was going to have to pick the layers. He decided that having some of all of the pieces might be fun. So that was settled.

"Now we have to go look at the venue. I'm not sure why it matters, but your mom said that we'd need a large place to accommodate all the people that might come. Also, after that, we have to decide on what to feed the masses." He asked her why they didn't start with the food. "I guess when you've had a full meal, the cake testing doesn't go as well. I don't know. I think that having a full meal means you have less room for cake. But that's just me."

The venue was the biggest place he'd ever seen. But then, since they were going to be married in late December, they would have to have everyone inside because of the cold. He didn't much care for the sterile look of the place, but the man showing them around said that it would be decorated and that it would be so much nicer. He didn't think that all the decorations in the world would make it look like a hospital operating room than it was now.

The second place they looked at wasn't able

to hold the number of people that they had invited. As the invitations were already sent out, they were already receiving RSVPs back that they would come. He was worried that even if they had their reception on an airstrip, there wouldn't be enough room. Something just then occurred to him.

"How are people going to know where to go for the reception if the invites have been sent out? I mean, usually, that's on them, correct?" Jade told him that a second invitation would be going out as soon as they picked a place. "Oh. I guess that makes sense."

"Since the wedding is going to be so soon, getting the invitations out as soon as possible was the best way to go. Also, the food that you're having at your wedding will be a chicken dish or beef. They can choose which one they'll want even though we have no idea what it might be." He thanked his mom. "You're so very welcome. Also, you and your brothers will have to have your tux cleaned and make sure that they fit you."

Jenson was getting nervous about the wedding. Not that he didn't want to marry Jade, but he wished they could have just eloped. But this was important to what their future would be. Having a large wedding would show that he was a man in love. His dad had told him that just yesterday.

Jade's phone rang, and she walked away to answer it. He wasn't sure about this building either, the third of the day, but he wasn't going to quibble about it. It didn't look as sterile as the first building, and this one was large enough to hold the guests without them being shoved against the walls. When Jade came back, he kissed her on the mouth. He loved having her close enough to do that whenever he wanted.

"That was VP Hardgrave. He said that he has a building that we can use that is right outside of Zanesville. It's not fancy, but it's huge and clean. He told me that if we were to go there now, he'd make sure that it was finished up, painted, and such before we needed it. What do you think?" He was all for it. "Good. Also, he said that he was impressed with your brother the other day. He met Clay at the job site and could not wait to meet the rest of his family. Also, Clay has top secret clearance, so he can work with me on some of the projects that I do on the side for the space program."

"He'll be thrilled." She said she thought so as well. "I'm ready anytime you are. Also, I'm going to have to get something to eat soon. Those little slices of food that we had aren't going to tie me over for much longer."

"You're just burning too many calories with all the sex we're having. Not that I mind, but I'm hungry and tired all the time now too." They went to the car holding hands. Mom and Hilda were going to go with them but in another car. Mom wanted to have dinner with dad, and Hilda had a few things that she had to take care of before tomorrow. "I thought we'd all have dinner together."

"Well, I guess we can invite the others to come into town. If they can." Jade told his mom that she'd like that. She missed having them all at the same table. "You say that now but after a while, you'll wish them to go away. I know I do on occasion."

The building was in a state of repair. But even with all the construction stuff lying around, he could see that it would be the perfect place for them to hold their reception. There was a bar going in as well as a kitchen that would work for the food being catered in. He was ready to say yes when Jade shook her head at him.

"We have to play it cool." He asked her in the same whispered voice why. "Because taking this building would mean that we owe the VP something in return. I hate owing anyone anything. But especially men in office."

"Okay, I can understand that." They continued on their tour of the building, the contractor pointing out things that were in the process of being taken care of. Jenson had also been able to ask a few questions about the building, and the contractor didn't have an answer. Jade winked at him. "It will be important to be able to use this building if there are enough bathrooms in the place. I think we're expecting over two hundred and fifty people at this thing. Also, it'll need heat. You didn't mention that when we arrived."

"The heat is going to be installed in the morning. It should have been here today, but there was a mix-up with the address. Also, air. Though I don't think you'll need that overly much in December." The contractor, Toby, he thought his name was laughed. "Also, an inspector is coming by in two days to make sure that the kitchen is up to standards."

All impressive but Jenson wasn't ready yet to seal the deal. Not without Jade giving him the okay. They did need to have the bathroom information as to how much the rental was going to be for the building, and, most importantly, would the building be finished in time? Jade's phone was ringing again when the contractor said he'd have to make a couple of calls.

Instead of walking away, she put it on speaker. It was the VP again, and he was answering their questions even as they were saying hello. His laughter sounded genuine, and it made Jenson smile. The man didn't laugh but sounded like a bullhorn going off.

"I never thought of the bathrooms. I'll have them expand it from two each to ten. It will be there for future use. Also, I will have it finished up by the end of the month." Jade said that they'd pay for the extra help that would be needed to get it done on time. "No need for that, Jade, honey. I'll see to it."

"I have to insist, sir. That way us using it won't seem like a bribe to us or from us. We'll pay the extra time, and that way, it could be considered an equal venture for us both." He didn't think that the man was going to agree, but he finally did. "Thank you.

That wasn't so hard, now was it?"

"No. Are you going to be like this all the time, Jade? Your poor future husband will be running for the hills if you are." Jenson told him that he was the luckiest man in the world and would never run from Jade. "I thought you'd say that. Also, if you don't mind, I'll be coming to the reception early and leaving early. I have to make sure that everything is going well for my two favorite people. The president might make it, but I wouldn't count on it. He's been busy with a few things going on overseas of late."

Jenson had been watching the events on the news. It was becoming a sticky situation. After hanging up with the VP, Jade asked him if he knew of a good construction company that didn't mind working with others. He did.

"My dad owns one. He used to work with the men until he broke his leg one summer. Mom told him that he was getting too important to her to lose him to a stupid accident. He goes to their working sites now but not to work. I'll call him and see what he can tell me."

Dad was excited to be able to help them out. The men would be in charge of the bathroom addition and anything else that the other contractors might need. When he approached the man in charge, he was happy to know that he'd already heard from his boss that there would be more people coming to help out. He had expressed his concerns about having the building finished on time. They set the date that it was needed, and everyone seemed to be happy about getting it finished for them.

His brothers were able to make it to dinner with them. He loved when they could all get together and have a meal as a family. Dad was talking to Barton about some things that he had going on, and the others were talking to Jade and Hilda about the wedding. He was blissfully happy that they all loved Jade as much as he did. Jenson thought that he could die a happy man right now but wasn't going to let that happen. He wanted to be a father, husband, and lover of the greatest woman on earth. Not necessarily in that order, either.

Taking her home after dinner, he thought of all the things that were going on in his life at the moment. He was working to become a congressman, getting married soon, and would be a father to his mother-in-law's child. And there wasn't a thing that he'd change about any of it.

Going up to bed when they got home, he was thinking of all the things that he had to do tomorrow. Letting it go in favor of sleeping, he nearly fell on his ass when he saw that Jade was in his bed. They'd been sneaking around having sex. Why? He had no idea, but it was thrilling for them. Getting into bed with her, she rolled over atop him and wrapped her arms around his body. His cock was hard, but he was exhausted. Thinking that he'd make love to her in the morning, Jenson was sound asleep in no time.

Jenson woke up coming hard. He had no idea what was going on until he realized that his cock was being bathed by Jade's mouth. Pulling her up to his body, he rolled her over and slammed his cock deep inside of her. Christ, he was coming again when she came screaming out his name.

Making love to her was gentler now. He ran his hands all over her body while nipping at her warm flesh. Her breasts were his favorite place to make love. Suckling each nipple until he moved down her body to explore other parts of her.

"Jenson, I need to explode with a climax. Stop fucking around and give it to me" He asked her what she needed. "I need for you to fill me while I scream. Fuck me. Just give me something so that I can come."

He didn't want to disappoint her, so he rolled to his back, taking her with him. When she sat up over him, Jenson thought that he'd been wrong about her beauty before. Her riding his cock like she was now was far beyond anything that he'd ever witnessed before.

While she fondled her breasts, he slid his finger over her clit. Jade cried out and begged him for more. Even as she came, screaming out her release, he rolled her over and fucked her hard and quick, losing himself in his climax.

He didn't remember falling asleep. Perhaps he just passed out. But when he woke with the sun shining in his room, he was alone in the big bed. Smiling about how he was sore in a few places, he decided that he was going to work on setting them up the best honeymoon anyone had ever had. Yes, sir, he told himself, he was going to have the best wife in the world, and he couldn't wait to show the world how happy he was.

Chapter 8

Clay found himself staring at his project more than working on it. It wasn't that he didn't have a great deal on his mind, but it kept drifting to Martin and how he'd not noticed that the man was ill. The very fact that he'd been able to hide it from him showed how well the man was at being able to fool anyone. He did wonder about his state of observation when he thought about how he'd been working with the man for so long and not noticed.

The slap to his back had him turning around to see who had hit him. When he saw Trevor there, he had to shake off his anger before speaking. That had been happening a great deal lately, too. His anger was quick to take over.

"What's wrong?" Clay told his brother that he'd hit him. "I'd been saying your name for the last ten minutes, and you were off someplace. It looked like you were getting more and more pissed off the longer you stood there. What's up with you lately?"

"I don't know. I feel pissed off all the time lately." Trevor told him that he'd noticed that he'd been avoiding them all lately and asked him if that was the reason. "Yes. I don't want to be in this mood, and one of you hurt me for being pissy. I've been hurt enough over the last few days."

"Yeah, mom told me about that guy. Scary thing, mental illness." He asked his brother what he wanted. "Okay, first of all, take it down a notch. I'm here because mom sent me. Don't bite my head off for no reason."

Clay had to stretch his neck to shake off hitting his brother. He walked away from him rather than engage to the point of anger again. It wasn't until his brother put his hands on his shoulders that he realized that something was seriously wrong. Clay sobbed that he was going to die.

"No, you're not. I'm going to take you to the

hospital, and we'll see what is going on. We'll just keep it between ourselves until we know anything. Maybe it's something as mild as an ear infection or something. We'll go, find out, and then we'll go from there." Agreeing to go was one of the hardest things he'd ever done. While he wanted to be angry with his brother, he knew that he'd just knock the shit out of him and take him anyway. He told him that. "You're so right on that. There is something off, and I'm worried about you. If it takes me knocking you out to get you help, then that's what I'm going to do."

In less time than he thought it should have taken, they were in the emergency department. There didn't seem to be anyone in the lobby, so he was taken right back to one of the rooms. After asking questions, most of which his brother answered for him, Clay could feel his temper getting the best of him, and he had to bite his tongue before speaking.

"I'd like to get a look at your entire body. I don't think that you have an ear infection, as your brother suggested, but it's hard to tell sometimes. Once we get the Cat Scan back, we'll have a better understanding, or at the very least, we'll be able to rule a few things out." He agreed with the doctor and was surprised that he was told he'd need an IV. "Also, Clay, I'd like to give you something to lower your blood pressure. It's higher than I'd like, and there isn't any sense in you suffering when you don't have to."

He was given meds to calm him down, and Clay felt his body relaxing. Once he was feeling good, he was taken to get his scan. Trevor said he'd be there in the room waiting for him when he returned. True to his word, he was sitting in the chair watching television when he was finished being scanned. Trevor asked him if he heard anything.

"I just got back." Counting to ten, he told his brother he was sorry. "I hate feeling like I'm ready to kill someone. All the fucking time."

"I'm glad that you agreed to come in, Clay. I'm seriously worried about you." Trevor held his hand while he dozed in and out of sleep. He knew, too, that he'd not be sleeping all that well and was glad for the meds to allow him to be out. When he woke once, Trevor was gone. He wasn't angry this time, but he did wonder where he'd gone. As soon as he came into the room, having gone to get something to eat, Clay realized that it had been a couple of hours since he'd had his scan.

"I was talking to one of the nurses in the cafeteria. She said that the hospital has been running so much better since Pauly was fired. Not to mention, she said that raises that they were promised are coming through and backdated. They're thrilled, as you can imagine." He said that he was happy for them all. "You're looking a little tense again. I'm wondering if the drugs are wearing off."

"I feel tense again. Like, I want to bite your head off. You've not done anything, yet here I lay wondering if I could snap your neck without having to move much." Trevor asked him if he wanted to kill him. "No. Not kill but just hurt you. That's not like me. Not at all."

"No, it's not." A nurse came in and gave him more of the same medication that he'd been given before. As he began to mellow out, the doctor came to speak to them. First, he asked if it was all right if Trevor was there. "He's responsible for me being here, so yes, I want him here."

"We found something on your brain. We'll have to run some tests on it to see what it is we're dealing with; however, I don't think it's cancer." Clay wanted his parents. Right now. Asking the doctor if he could hold off on talking to them until their parents arrived. He nodded. "I was going to suggest that, but I didn't want to step on your toes. You were smart to agree with your brother about coming in here, Clay. As I said, I don't know what we're dealing with right now, but it'll help you to have your family here to help you cope."

Mom and dad showed up in twenty minutes. They'd been out, going to dinner, when Trevor called. He'd not realized that he'd called his brothers until they started showing up one at a time. Even Jade and her mom came into the room with them. Eventually, they were moved to another, larger room, and everyone, including him where seated around a large conference table. His scans were put on a monitor so that everyone could see them.

Clay could see the mass in his head. It was just above his ear and seemingly large. He felt his anger and other emotions begin to take hold of him when his mom put her hand on his. That was all it took for him to regain control. Christ, he was a mess right now.

"As you can see here, there is a mass along the left side of his face. The darkness around it is approximately two centimeters. When he's stressed, as he was when he came in, it presses against the amygdala triggering his emotions. It could well have been fear or any other emotion, but anger is the one that is making its presents known to all of you around him." Jade asked him why no one had seen it when he'd been in the hospital yesterday. "I don't think they were looking for anything other than to make sure that there were no cracks in his skull. Which there isn't. But I went and had a look at the other scan that they did, and it's visible. We're lucky that Trevor here knew something was off about his brother and made sure that he was brought in."

Clay looked over at Jade when she said his name quietly. Clay felt the tears of stress start to roll down his cheeks. He told her that he was beyond terrified right now and didn't know what to do.

"You're going to do as your told, and we'll get you fixed up." He nodded. "No, you don't believe me. Say it, Clay. You're going to be just fine, and we'll all work together to help you with this. All right?"

"Yes. I'm going to be just fine, and I'll do what

I'm told." She kissed him on the cheek. "I needed that, Jade. Thank you. I just thought I was going through a phase or something."

"You're much too young to be hitting your menopause, Clay." He told her that he thought it was a mid-life crisis when you were male. "If you give me any shit, you're going to wish for it to be a crisis and not another injury."

Clay couldn't help it. He laughed. Drawing attention to himself in the process, he waved the others back to the conversations. For the first time since he started having these unwelcomed thoughts, he did believe that he was going to be all right.

"I have a surgeon coming in tomorrow to evaluate you, Clay. I'm going to put you on a clear liquid until midnight. Then if he thinks that it's what I'm telling you, he'll do the operation at that time. While it's not life or death that it happens soon, I'm sure you and your family want to get this over with so that you can get on the mend." He was all for that and agreed with the doctor. "All right then. We'll set you up in a room tonight on the surgical floor then you'll be taken back there after recovery. You're going to be fine, young man. We'll keep you on the medications that you've been taking so that you can rest well."

Trevor left him before his parents did. They wanted to spend the night, but the doctor said they'd be better in their beds tonight so that they'd be rested up. Clay didn't want to argue with him about someone staying with him, but his parents were going to need to sleep. He even gave them a little bit of a relaxant to take when they got home.

It was nearing midnight when he'd had all the tests that he'd need in the morning. Trevor came into the room with a knapsack. Taking out an air mattress as well as a sleeping bag and pillow, Clay cried for nearly an hour before he was able to get his emotions in check.

"I came here to see you through this big brother. I'm not going to leave you here by yourself, no matter what the doctor says. I've eaten so I'd not tempt you with food and had plenty of drink. I'm staying right here until you're ready to bust out of this place and head home."

The nurses were in and out of his room. A couple of times, he woke up to Trevor talking to them. By the time the sun was coming up, he'd already had his gown changed out and his hair put in some kind of netting. The doctor had seen his scan and saw no reason to put off the surgery. His family came in when they were giving him something more to make him relax. Clay could barely form words but thought he'd gotten it across that he was glad they were there.

Being wheeled down to the surgical floor, Jade stopped them before he could get on the elevator. She kissed him on the mouth quickly and told him to behave himself, or she'd be the one cutting him open. He winked at her, about all he could manage at the moment, and she smiled. By the time he was put onto the table to be operated on, Clay was feeling his tension build back up.

"No need for that, young man. I've got you. And I've done this kind of surgery a few times. You're in good hands." He nodded and asked how long it would take. "You'll never know anything other than you'll close your eyes, and when you open them, it'll be over. Just you let me do the worrying, and you relax."

"Nervous." He nodded over his shoulder, and Clay turned to look. "You have pretty eyes. I bet the rest of you are pretty too."

The woman laughed. Wiping his chin, she told him that he was drooling and that she was going to bump up his meds. Clay felt the medication drift over him so much stronger than it had when he'd been getting medications from the nurse. He must have spoken out loud because beautiful eyes spoke to him.

"I have the good stuff in here. You just breathe in and out, Mr. Strong, and you'll be sleeping better than you have in a long time." He tried to ask her what her name was. "Lizzy. Short of Elizabeth. And I don't usually date the people that I have to work on."

"Did I ask you out?" She nodded, and he felt himself drifting. It was getting hard for him to focus on anything until she told him to stop fighting it and let it work. "I'd like to have dinner with you soon."

As soon as he closed his eyes. He didn't know what they were giving him, but it did feel like the good stuff. He was going to invest it in when he was awake, he told himself before there was nothing left of his thoughts.

~*~

Jenson listened to the surgeon as he explained what he'd found when he'd cut open Clay. The doctor, Doctor Jamison Fields, said that Clay would be just fine after he woke up and that he would be going home tomorrow so long as he would do as he was told. It was their mom that said he would be. Then Jade said she'd knock him around if he tried anything stupid.

"Having family support will be good for him. For all of you. As I was saying, it was fairly simple to remove. I looked to make sure that I got it all and sent it off for testing. I don't believe that there is anything to worry about, but I don't like to take chances with something on the brain." Mom asked him what would happen if it turned out to be cancerous. "Let's not build bridges that we're not needing right now. Let's just focus on what we do know. He's a young, healthy man. Clay has a good support system, and we're going to leave it at that."

He wondered if the doctor knew that it wasn't going to happen, to let it wait. Clay was his younger brother, and the very fact that he'd had to have surgery bothered him on all kinds of levels. Jenson wanted to talk to Trevor and ask him what made him bring Clay in. Trevor started speaking almost as if he heard his question.

"When I went to see him in his office the other day, he was pissed off beyond what I thought was right for him. When I told him I was worried about him, he seemed to be relieved that someone was going to help him. I've never seen Clay like he's been for the last few months. And it was getting worse. I have to admit, when he agreed to go to the ER with me, I doubled my worrying." Doctor Fields said that the headaches alone would have been crushing to him. And having his head hit the way that he did might have made it worse. "I'm just glad that he agreed to go in. I told him if he hadn't, then I had plans to knock the crap out of him and take him anyway."

"Good for you, young man." They talked about other things that were going to be happening with Clay. It was unknown how long the mass had been there, but he explained that it might take him a while for the damage that had been done to go away. Jade asked him what sort of damage. "His hearing would have been affected. I'm not sure how much, but it was pressing against other parts of the area. Clay might have lost a bit of his taste. With the brain, it's difficult to tell what may have been giving him trouble when the mass started to enlarge."

Jenson didn't want to hear anything more, so he left the room. A nurse asked him if he'd like to sit in recovery with Clay while he waited for him to wake. That was the best news that he could have heard all day. After getting dressed in a gown and mask, he went into the room with Clay and sat by his bed.

"You can touch him so long as you're gloved, Mr. Strong." He told her to call him Jenson. "I can do that. I was in surgery with your brother. I can answer questions you might have now if you'd like. I will admit that he asked me out. He said that I had pretty eyes."

He looked at her. "They're very pretty. A sort of lavender, right?" She nodded and adjusted something on his IV. "I hate that this had to happen to him. Clay and I have always been close, and this tears me up that he's going through this."

"Yes, he is. However, he's not going through it alone. A family around a person who is ill or had surgery will make them feel better quicker. He'll depend on you all a great deal, but the trick is for him to be able to take care of himself too." He asked her if she was going to go out with him. "I've been thinking about it since he asked me. Do you have any objections to him going out to dinner with a surgical nurse?"

"So long as he's happy, I could care less if you had fifty kids and twenty-five ex-husbands." She laughed with him. "No, really, I don't care whom he dates. We're all good men, and I do not doubt that he'll treat you like a princess."

"Thank you, Jenson. I might go if he remembers that he asked me. Sometimes it's the juice they get before surgery that makes them less inhibited about asking people out. We'll just have to wait and see what he wants." Jenson had a feeling that Clay would remember and want to date this woman frequently. He liked her and could see why Clay had asked her out.

As he sat with Clay while he slept, he told him everything that he could remember about his surgery. He even told him that Jade was going to be upset with him if he didn't do as he was told. Then Jenson laughed.

"I'm sure that mom and dad will be on your

ass too about doing what you're told. I've never seen them so stressed out before. But it's all good news like we were hoping for, and we couldn't ask for a better surgeon." He then told him about the pretty surgical assistant. "Lizzy was just in here. She told me that you asked her out. She'll go out with you if you remember to ask her again. I'll try to drop some hints to you when you wake up. I like her if that makes a difference. Not that it should, but I do."

Jenson watched as the nurses came in and out of the room. He was hooked up to a blood pressure monitor that he watched diligently. It never seemed to rise very high, for which he was glad. After they left him again, he spoke to Clay.

"Thanksgiving is tomorrow. We completely forgot about it. Mom said that when you got home, she'd make sure that she had everything ready for us all to have a meal together. Then after that, Christmas. After that, I'm going to be married."

He thought about all the plans that were taking place to get himself married to his fast-becoming best friend. Telling Clay about the venue building, he was glad that they'd paid for the other repairs going on. To make it seem less like it was repayable favor.

"I'm not unhappy about the big wedding. However, I wouldn't recommend it to anyone that doesn't have a great deal of money. The food alone is costing more than I paid for my first year of law school. Mom is so excited to have this going on that I find that I can't tell her no to things that I don't care about. I also think that Jade is having fun planning it." He thought about the gifts that he was going to give his brothers for standing up with him. "No pressure here, but unless you want to be standing up there with a stranger, I'd suggest to Jade that you can find your date." His dad came into the room with him, dressed like he was, and sat down.

"I can't take any more of the information that the doctor is giving us," Jenson told his dad that was why he'd come here. "It's a good place to be. Are you talking to him about the surgery?"

"Not really. I've been rambling about different things. Mostly nothing that matters at all." Dad nodded. "The other day, I heard mom talking about a cruise. When was the last time you took one with her? I think it's been too long, even if it was only a month ago."

"I was thinking that same thing just this

morning. That was where we were headed when Trevor called us. To make plans." Jenson told him about the honeymoon that he was planning with Jade. "Oh, she'll love that, Jenson. A tour of Europe? I've not been there in ages. I'm not going with the two of you, but I am going to think about planning a trip with your mother soon."

The two of them talked to each other and Clay. When the nurse came in to take his vitals again, she told them that he'd be going to his room soon. That they were lowering his medication so that he'd wake up. He asked if he'd be in any pain when he did.

"No. He'll still have a lot of medications in his system. Getting him to wake up will help us determine if there were any short or long-term issues with him being operated on. Also, with the medication that he was given to put him under." Dad asked if they thought that would happen. "I can't tell you for sure, Mr. Strong. But as the doctor pointed out to you, he's young and healthy. You have to believe that he's going to be just fine."

"We will." When she left them, Dad looked over at him. "It's difficult to watch your child be in pain. Even more so when you can't do anything about it. He'll be fine, I'm sure of it, but no parent wants to see their child hurting like this."

"I don't want it either." About twenty minutes later, Clay turned to look at him. He couldn't talk yet. His face was tightly bandaged, but he put out his hand to dad, and he took it. Watching dad cry while he told Clay that he was going to be fine hurt his heart too. Seeing his big strong dad crying hurt him deep within his heart.

The surgeon came in to remove some of the bandages. Mostly it was the one that was wrapped around his head. When he cut that away, Clay could move his mouth. But he was cautioned about doing too much. It would make him sore.

He would doze in and out while talking to them. Clay would ask the same questions over and over — did they find any cancer? Was he going to be all right? Things that they didn't have an answer for yet, but Clay didn't seem to mind. Then he asked about Lizzy. After explaining to dad who she was, he told his brother what she'd said.

"Why would I care?" Clay dozed off with the promise from him to be awakened if she came by. They were moving him down to his room when he saw Lizzy standing by the nurse's station talking. Clay woke up and saw her. Smiling at her, he reached for her hand. "There is my pretty date."

She laughed and asked him how medicated he was. Clay took her hand into his and didn't let it go when he fell asleep again. Every time she tried to take it back, he'd wake and take her hand into his.

"We'll have dinner." She asked him if he was hungry. "Not really, but I will be. I'm betting if you kiss me right now, I'll be so much better."

"I can't do that, sir. I'm on duty until midnight. However, I will come by your room to see you after I'm done. I'm not saying you'll be getting a kiss, but I will go by to see how you're doing." He thanked her. When he was in his room again, Jenson thought that the pain was making itself known to him. As soon as he was moved over to his bed, Clay asked for pain medication. That alone told him that he was hurting badly.

Lizzy did come by to see Clay, but he was still in and out of it. He didn't wake up to talk to her, but she asked him to make sure that Clay knew that she'd kissed him when he did wake. Dad thought it was funny that Clay was doing better with women knocked out than his other brothers were doing fully awake.

"What are you talking about, dad? Clay has always had an easy time getting dates. I swear to you, he's been practicing his moves since Charlene Bauer kissed him in preschool when he was five." The two of them laughed. "You should go on home, dad. I've got this. He's going to be released sometime tomorrow, and I know that you and mom are going to be dealing with him. Trevor is coming in later to stay with him all night too."

"I'm so proud of my boys." Emotional, Jenson told his dad that they had good role models. "I never thought that there was anything wrong with Clay. I have to admit that I was ready to knock him around a bit when he made your mother cry. But he came back into the house and hugged her. To know that he was dealing with this makes me feel like a fool for not making sure he was all right."

"I don't think that anyone of us knew what to look for. Trevor had been gone for a week, and when he returned, he saw it. We were too close to him to see what was happening." Dad said that he should have checked. "You can't check on us whenever we're having a bad day and think that it's something seriously wrong. As I said, we were all too close to him to see anything. The doctor did say that it had grown. There isn't any telling how long it was there before Trevor came home."

"I know that. I do. But it doesn't make me feel any better knowing that he was suffering." Dad stood up. "I think that I will go home. I told your mom that I'd be home before too much longer. She's worried, as you can well imagine, and I want to be there for her too."

Jenson hugged his dad tightly and told him to drive carefully home. Once he was seated with Clay again, Trevor showed up. He'd brought an extra sleeping bag for him, saying that they'd take turns watching him.

"You think we have to watch his every move?" He said that Jade and mom both made him promise that one of them would be awake all the time. "They're worried. But I don't know that I could sleep very well without knowing that he's being watched over. This scared the shit out of me."

"Me too. When he agreed to go to the hospital, I knew that something was wrong. He's like you in that respect. Stubborn as all hell." Jenson said he didn't think of himself as stubborn. "You're not now that you've met Jade. You were close all the time to losing your shit. But differently than Clay had been. You were just pissed off. He wanted to kill. He told me that. Scared the crap right out of me when he said he wanted to snap my neck."

"I was hurting." Clay didn't move when he spoke from the bed, but they both asked him if he was all right. "Yes. Better but still in pain. But not from the mass or whatever it was. Do you know yet? I'm not nearly awake right now, but if you tell me, I'll try to remember what you say."

"We won't know anything until later. When they come to tell us, do you want us to wake you?" Clay said no, he wanted to rest. "I can understand that. The nurse that was in here before Trevor arrived said they might keep you an extra day. Depending on how well you do tonight. I'd stay if I were you. They're not going to be giving you the good stuff when you leave."

"Right now, I think I'd have to agree with you on that. I'm sore, like I said, but it seems like my body is hurting too. More than likely, I think it's because

I was so tense all the time." Clay couldn't yawn yet, but he did try. "I'm going to sleep now. See if you two can keep your mouth closed for a while, and we'll talk tomorrow."

Telling his brothers good night, Jenson stepped into the hall to call his parents. Telling them that he'd been talking to them but still in pain. He could tell that they were both relieved to hear that, and he told them that he loved them.

"We both love you too, Jenson. You stay with Clay and Trevor, and we'll see you sometime in the morning." Telling them good night, he hung up. When he went into the room, Trevor was in the chair, and his sleeping bag was on the mattress. He told him it was his turn to watch over him.

Letting him take the watch was all right with him. Jenson messaged Jade to tell her that he loved her as well. Jenson laid down. He was exhausted and worn out. Tomorrow was going to be a much better day. He knew it.

Before You Go...

HELP AN AUTHOR

write a review

THANK YOU!

Share your voice and help guide other readers to these wonderful books. Even if it's only a line or two, your reviews help readers discover the author's books so they can continue creating stories that you'll love. Log in to your favorite retailer and leave a review. Thank you.

AWARD WINNING, BESTSELLING AUTHOR

Kathi Barton, a winner of the Pinnacle Book Achievement award as well as a best-selling author on Amazon and All Romance books, lives in Nashport, Ohio, with her husband, Paul. When not creating new worlds and romance, Kathi and her husband enjoy camping and going to auctions. She can also be seen at county fairs with her husband, who is an artist and potter.

Her muse, a cross between Jimmy Stewart and Hugh Jackman, brings her stories to life for her readers in a way that has them coming back time and again for more. Her favorite genre is paranormal romance, with a great deal of spice. You can visit Kathi on line and drop her an email if you'd like. She loves hearing from her fans. aaronskiss@gmail.com.

Follow Kathi on her blog: http://kathisbartonauthor.blogspot. com/